"This—us—" he said bluntly, "won't work here."

"I think you're worried about nothing," she said tightly. "I'm not looking for romance, and if I was, I wouldn't look to you."

Color flared on his cheekbones. "I could make you eat your words."

"That wasn't a dare, Dante, just a statement of fact. You like to think you've got me—and life—all figured out. Well, you don't. You might be able to control yourself, but can't control others, and you certainly can't control me. I'm here for one reason and one reason only—to work."

"You are attracted to me," he insisted.

"Just like I'm attracted to a thousand other men. But I don't chase them and I don't hop into bed with them. So you can relax, Count, you're safe with me."

Suddenly he was moving toward her and lifting her to her feet. Just his hands on her arms made her shiver, but when his leg bumped her knee, wedging her feet apart, she gasped for air.

"What was that?" he murmured. "Were you eating your words, maybe?"

In Dante's Debt
by
Jane Porter

Look for the next exciting chapter
in this new series, on sale next month.

Lazaro's Revenge #2304

Coming in February
Harlequin Presents®

Jane Porter

IN DANTE'S DEBT

THE Galván Brides

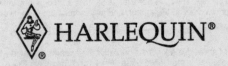
HARLEQUIN®

TORONTO • NEW YORK • LONDON
AMSTERDAM • PARIS • SYDNEY • HAMBURG
STOCKHOLM • ATHENS • TOKYO • MILAN • MADRID
PRAGUE • WARSAW • BUDAPEST • AUCKLAND

For Tessa. A wizard and a brilliant editor.

ISBN 0-373-12298-5

IN DANTE'S DEBT

First North American Publication 2003.

Copyright © 2001 by Jane Porter.

This edition published by arrangement with Harlequin Books S.A.

Visit us at www.eHarlequin.com

Printed in U.S.A.

CHAPTER ONE

"A HALF million dollars?" Daisy Collingsworth repeated incredulously, her lips curving tightly, heart thumping with sickening speed. "You might as well slit my wrists, Count Galván, I'd bleed faster that way."

A trio of sleek glossy thoroughbreds pounded past, jockeys sitting high in the saddle, hooves kicking up fine pink-brown dust.

But Dante Galván ignored the yearlings in training. "I don't want to kill you. I just want my share."

"The *lion's* share," she retorted fiercely, grinding the heels of her boots into the soft racing track dirt, unable to fathom how fate, and her father's mistakes, had so completely turned their lives upside down. This should never have happened. Not in a thousand years. The family farm was not negotiable. Never had been. Never would be.

But he clearly was unmoved by her argument. "I only take what is mine."

She suddenly pictured him as a lion, a massive glorious leo sunning on a rock while a half dozen lionesses loyally, happily did his work.

The mental picture infuriated her. Yes, he was Dante Galván, the son of one of her father's former business associates—an associate notorious for underhanded business practices—but that had no weight with her. She wasn't about to be knuckled under. "I will get a lawyer and fight you all the way."

"Lawyers are expensive, Miss Collingsworth, and in this case even an excellent lawyer will be a waste of money."

Her lips parted to interrupt but he held up a finger, momentarily silencing her.

"And if I might use a cliché," he continued smoothly, the expression on his handsome face genial, downright friendly. "Even with a good attorney, you have no legal leg on which to stand. Your father signed a contract. My stables provided the stallion. Your mare delivered a foal. It's time you paid the stud fee."

She didn't need to look at the contract to remember the outrageous amount the Galváns had charged them for the stallion's stud fee. It was so outrageous she'd actually laughed out loud the first time she'd seen the statement. "Nearly half a million dollars, Count Galván? Can we please be serious? No stallion is worth a half-million-dollar stud fee."

"Your father seemed to think so."

She colored, her face burning in hot fierce bands. "My father—" She broke off, swallowed hard, fighting the wave of nausea that threatened to overtake her. After a moment she felt calm enough to try again. "My father wasn't thinking clearly."

It was as close to the truth as she could admit. Anything else would be revealing too much of their own personal tragedy, and that she'd never do, especially not to a man as calculating and self-serving as Count Dante

Galván. He was, she thought contemptuously, no different from his greedy, manipulative father. Nothing like a chip off the old block.

His eyes suddenly narrowed, his expression subtly hardening. "I'm not interested in excuses. Your father knew what he was doing."

"Call a spade a spade, Count Galván! Your father knew exactly what he was doing. You know how much my father looked up to him—"

"If you hope to appeal to my heart," he interrupted curtly, "you're going about it the wrong way. There is no love lost between my father and me."

"Even though he's gone?"

"Especially now that he's gone. Death doesn't excuse or forgive incompetence."

"My goodness, you're cold."

"Not entirely." His hands went to his hips, pushing aside the soft suede coat, and he half-smiled, a small ironic smile. "I'm not immune to the plight of a beautiful young woman facing bankruptcy and eviction. I do feel for you and understand perfectly why your father sent you to meet with me."

His lips were stretched into a smile, and yet she'd never seen more teeth or such an impression of a snarl. He looked like a big cat about to take down its prey. Her heart thumped double hard. "And why is that?"

"You're to butter me up, sweet-talk your way into more time, perhaps a better deal?"

She felt herself blush. "If my father wanted to butter you up, he would have sent Zoe. My sister is the sugar in the family. I'm the vinegar."

Dante Galván threw his dark head back and laughed, melting the tension from his shoulders, easing the lines from his mouth and eyes. He suddenly looked lazy, relaxed, completely at ease. "So you're not trying to butter me up? You're not going to ask for favors?"

His supple brown leather coat hung open over an oatmeal-colored knit sweater. The sweater clung to the hard curved planes of his shoulders and chest. He was gorgeous. And there was nothing worse than a man who knew he looked good.

Daisy cast his dark sun-streaked hair a critical glance. Just look at him! He wore his hair long, well past his collar. She saw the way he'd ruffled it earlier as he sighed, feigning boredom. What an ego. And now he was standing here, licking his chops, anticipating his money.

Fury surged through her, fury and indignation. He, who had so much, now wanted to strip them of the little they had left.

"I wouldn't call it a favor," she said flatly. "But we do need time. We don't have a half million dollars in the savings account. We don't even have five thousand dollars in the savings account. But we can work out a payment plan—"

"Your father said that a year ago but there's been no payment. There's been nothing at all."

"I sent you a check last month."

"Yes, and it bounced."

His sarcasm made her wince, and her stomach plummeted, a speedy free fall that left her cold and clammy.

Deeply embarrassed by the reminder, she felt the blood drain from her face.

The bounced check had been an awful, ungodly and yet ridiculous mistake, a mistake she rarely made with finances. Somehow last month, in her hurry to get bills paid on time, she'd failed to record a cash withdrawal from the ATM in downtown Lexington. The cash withdrawal hadn't been huge, but it was large enough to insure that the check to the Galváns wouldn't clear. And it didn't.

Daisy cursed herself yet again, bitterly heaping blame on her head.

If she'd only double-checked her ATM slips, if she'd only waited an extra day before mailing off the payment to the Galváns, none of this would have happened.

If she hadn't made that silly error, Count Galván would have accepted the delinquent but legitimate payment, and the Collingsworths would finally be working their way out of debt.

Instead Count Galván was here, and he wanted blood.

Daisy drew herself tall and met his cynical gaze head-on. "The check would have cleared the next day. If you'd given the check a chance to clear. But you wouldn't do that."

He didn't look the least bit remorseful. "No, I wouldn't. I learned my lesson. You weren't serious about settling the debt. You're playing games—"

"Not true!" Daisy couldn't help herself. The words flew out of her mouth before she could stop them. An immediate blush followed, her face burning from brow to chin, her cheeks feverishly hot. "It's not like that at all."

His lashes suddenly dropped, his gaze intently examining her flushed cheeks and pinched lips. His voice lowered, too, taking on an almost caressing tone. "Then how is it, Daisy Collingsworth? Can you explain it to me?"

With his words he was asking for an explanation, but his eyes were asking for something else, something entirely different. He was subtly shifting the focus from business to personal, from work to her. She felt a bubble of warmth rise inside her, adrenaline and nerves. She'd never dealt with anyone like Dante Galván before, didn't know the first thing about how to handle a man like him.

She drew a ragged breath, nails biting into her palms. "I can cut you another check right now for last month's and this month's payment. I promise it will never happen again. You have my word."

Count Galván's leather-coated shoulders shifted, a small, apologetic shrug. "I can't accept that. I'm sorry."

It felt as though he'd punched her in the ribs. Daisy sucked in air, trying not to flinch. He had no idea how hard she'd worked this past year, no idea the sacrifices made to free up enough cash to give him one month's payment, much less two.

Jackass. Her eyes burned but she held the sting of tears back. He was such a jackass. He was so rich, so successful that he didn't know what it was like to count every little penny, to scrape together loose change, to deny oneself the most basic of expenses to free up every dollar possible.

For what?

A horse farm. A bankrupt four-generations family horse farm.

The moment Daisy thought it, she felt worse than before. She didn't hate the farm. She loved the farm. The farm was her life. It meant everything to her—the horses, the land, the farm buildings—this was home and to hell with Dante Galván if he thought he could take it from her.

Daisy tightened the muscles in her legs, locked her knees and pressed down through her heels, rooting her to the soil. "My word might mean nothing to you, but our cash should. You want to be paid, I'm telling you that you'll be paid. I'll cut the check now and accompany you to the bank."

"What about next month? What happens in thirty days?"

He was trying to bait her but she wouldn't do it. He wasn't going to get another rise out of her. "You'll be paid. Promptly."

"And the month after that?"

"Stop it." She didn't snap, but she wasn't smiling, either. She was too tired to do this. She didn't have the patience. Her father had been particularly difficult last night, and instead of waking Zoe as they'd agreed, Daisy let her younger sister sleep, knowing that Zoe needed her rest. But the generous gesture last night meant that Daisy was worn out this morning and Count Galván's patronizing attitude was wearing her raw.

His lips, full and overtly sensual, twisted. "Miss Collingsworth, I'm not trying to be rude. I'm simply trying to make the point that I can't afford to wait to be paid. Your farm is clearly struggling. If we don't settle the debt now, I think it's highly unlikely it will ever be settled.''

She was tall, five ten without her boots, but he was a good head taller. She jerked her chin up, her gaze colliding with his. "You really do like to hit below the belt.''

"Never with a woman, especially not with a woman like you.''

She averted her head, half closing her eyes, denying the honey warmth flooding her limbs.

His husky pitch did as much damage to her nerves as his words. He couldn't have meant anything by that, and if he did, she wouldn't let herself feel flattered. "We own the house free and clear. We're not about to lose the house—''

"But you've taken out second and third loans on the property itself. You're behind in payments to the bank.''

How did he know that? She felt sick to her stomach. "But the bank won't foreclose. I'm working on a payment plan with them.''

"Just like you've been working on a payment plan with me.''

For a moment she almost thought she was going to lose her breakfast, throw up her coffee and cold cereal all over his polished leather loafers. But she clamped her jaw tight, ground her teeth and held back the sick wave of nausea.

Daisy couldn't imagine a more awful torture. She, with all her pride, forced to endure his condescension and pity. The poor Collingsworths...those hapless, helpless down-on-their-luck Collingsworths...

No. She wouldn't buy into it. They were struggling but they weren't down and out. She'd find a way out of this. She'd get her family through this. One way or another.

Daisy pushed up the brim of her taupe cowboy hat, and her long blond ponytail fell forward, slipping over her shoulder in a silvery sheen. "Count Galván, I realize we owe you nearly a half million dollars for the stud fee and I realize two small monthly payments seem like a drop in the bucket, but I'm attempting to settle this debt. However, you won't work with me, and I can't make you work with me, but I can consult an attorney and get some legal advice—"

"Advice?" His tone turned deceptively soft.

"Regarding harassment," she hurriedly continued, trying to ignore the fact that his cheekbones had hardened, the high curve turning to granite as his lips compressed.

"*Muneca*, you don't want to take me to court."

His husky voice trickled down her spine like fingertips, and she shivered inwardly, more deeply affected than she'd admit. "I can file Chapter Eleven. We'd be protected while we reorganized our debt. You wouldn't see a penny for a long, long time."

He didn't say anything. He simply stared at her, a mixture of disgust and amazement lighting his eyes. She'd surprised him.

Daisy wondered why she didn't feel more victorious. In truth, she felt a little afraid. Only fools turned the

Galváns into adversaries. The Galváns were incredibly powerful people. Her father had always tried so hard to keep the peace with the late Tino Galván.

Thankfully Dante's cellular phone began to ring, and he fished inside his leather coat, retrieving the phone from an inner pocket. The phone was minuscule, barely larger than a credit card. Of course he'd carry the newest form of technology. Nothing but the most modern and most expensive for Count Dante Galván.

He turned away to take the call but Daisy watched him converse, his dark head tipped in concentration, lashes lowered to conceal his expression. Suddenly he looked at her from beneath his lashes and caught her staring.

He lifted his eyebrows slightly as if to say, "Well? Do you like what you're seeing?" and Daisy blushed deeply, a frisson of warmth bursting to life within her. She hated that she even found him interesting. He shouldn't be interesting to her. He was shallow, superficial, spoiled. He—but no, she didn't want to think about him, didn't want to waste even a second on him.

Abruptly Daisy moved away, walking on stiff legs to the edge of the track. Drawing a deep breath, she leaned against the painted fence railing and waited for the trio of horses to round the bend.

The thudding hooves shook the ground, sending a rumbling sensation through her boots and into her legs. She watched as the horses galloped closer, and Daisy moved near the fence to get the best view possible. She held her breath as the horses thundered past, the jockeys a blur of red and yellow in their training jackets.

Oh, how beautiful they are.

For a blissful moment she forgot everything—her father, the debt, Dante Galván—too immersed in joy.

Her gaze clung to the yearlings, enthralled by the vision of long legs flying, arched satiny necks, tails sailing. Her horses, her farm, her future.

"You file Chapter Eleven and you might as well close Collingsworths' doors." His voice came from behind her. "Horses are big business, particularly in Kentucky. You don't play with people's investments."

She snapped upright. She hadn't realized he'd finished his call, nor heard him approach.

"I understand," she answered tightly, irritated by his superciliousness. His superiority grated on her. How could he think he was more virtuous simply because he had money and they had none? "But people around here also know the Collingsworths are honest. We've been in business more than eighty years. We've hit rough patches before and pulled through."

He didn't immediately speak, and she couldn't bring herself to turn and face him. He was wreaking havoc on her nerves. She definitely had lost the upper hand.

The silence seemed to last forever. At length he spoke. "Where is your father?"

His tone had lost its brusqueness. He sounded almost conciliatory. She turned slightly, glanced at him. "He's retired."

"I wouldn't call it a good time for him to retire."

"In our business there's never a good time to retire."

His jaw tightened, deep grooves forming along his mouth. "But he's left this…disaster…to you?"

"This disaster is our farm, and yes, I manage the farm now, so unlucky for you, you're going to have to deal with me."

"Oh, I'd say lucky me," he corrected softly.

It was the last thing she expected him to say. Daisy flooded hot, cold and began to shiver.

She could deal with sarcasm, deal with intimidation, but she couldn't handle this—this...

Suggestive sort of foreplay. Or whatever it was. She'd never been particularly sexual or confident about herself as a woman. She knew she was smart and strong, but not...

Daisy flushed and ground her teeth, digging her hands into the back pockets of her jeans to hide her trembling. He was making her incredibly self-conscious, and suddenly she didn't know how to handle this conversation anymore.

In the old days she would have thrown a punch. It was the way she grew up solving problems but she hadn't thrown a punch in years, not since Tommy Wilcox had made fun of thirteen-year-old Zoe's braces and she left Tommy with a black eye, bruised ego and a new, healthy respect for the Collingsworth sisters.

What Daisy wouldn't give to teach Dante Galván a similar lesson.

But she was done with her fighting days, done acting the part of a rough-and-tumble tomboy. At twenty-four she knew a quick temper wouldn't solve the problems facing her family. Only a cool head would get them out of this crisis.

Dante glanced at his watch and with a sigh shook his

sleeve down, covering the gleam of gold on his wrist. "As much as I'm enjoying this little tête-à-tête, a problem has come up in Buenos Aires. I have to return to the hotel to handle this, but I will be back, Miss Collingsworth. Sooner than you think."

He couldn't be pleasant. Not even if he tried. But Daisy forced a smile even though it made her jaw ache. "Is that a promise, Count Galván, or a threat?"

He laughed, and the early morning sunlight cascaded over him, forming a halo around his dark head, creating the impression of impossible strength and energy. "You're not going to get rid of me that easily."

Again his eyes smoldered, his expression both personal and tangible. He made her feel so aware of herself, and aware of him. He made her realize that they were very different people and somehow he made it seem like an intriguing premise. "I'll be back later today."

Daisy swallowed hard, quivered inwardly, stung by the spark of heat, and took an instinctive step backward. "I've appointments until noon," she said. He didn't need to know that she'd be home, helping her father with his morning routine.

"We can meet after lunch then. I want to go over your books, see the records."

"Those are private."

"Daisy, I'm trying to keep this civil. It doesn't have to be war—"

"Afraid you'd lose?"

His smile was small. He gave his head a brief, benevolent if regretful shake. "No. You'd lose. And you'd lose everything."

Daisy's heart pounded as she drove the short distance home. His parting words filled her with dread. It wasn't that his tone had been cruel. Far from it. He'd actually spoken most gently. Rather, she was troubled by the stark realization that he was *right*. Legally, morally, financially. They owed him.

She parked the old work truck in front of the house and climbed the four front steps leading to the covered porch. Stepping through the front door of the two-story Victorian farmhouse, she smelled the faint tang of the lemon oil and the musky spice of antique English roses, varieties planted by her mother over twenty years ago.

She yanked off her hat and shook her long hair loose from its ponytail, the heavy mass reaching the dip in her back. She tossed the hat on the stair banister, passed the mirror without giving it a glance and headed straight for the kitchen.

Twenty-year-old Zoe turned from the sink where she was washing pots and pans, her blond hair twisted into a knot on top of her head. Even though they were four years apart, people often mistook them for twins.

"More calls," Zoe said softly, lavender-blue eyes wide with apprehension. "Five of them today."

Creditors were always calling. They started early, sometimes before seven. Daisy's stomach knotted, but she forced a smile, wanted to somehow reassure her sister. "It'll be all right, Zoe. I'll call them back this afternoon."

Straddling one of the kitchen's ladder-back chairs, Daisy sat down and rubbed her temples, trying not to be overwhelmed as the mountain of worries kept getting bigger. "How's Dad this morning?"

Zoe leaned against the sink and slowly wiped her sudsy hands dry. A long blond tendril had slipped from the knot and fluttered against her cheek. "Not so good. He's been asking for Mom." She stared at her hands, rubbing the dish towel across one hand and then the other.

Daisy watched her sister methodically rub the towel, her hands constantly moving, her anxiety palpable.

Finally Zoe looked up, her eyes wide and wet with tears she wouldn't shed. "I never know what to tell him anymore."

Zoe shouldn't have to go through this, Daisy argued silently. She'd never even had the chance to go to college or get out on her own. She'd jumped from teenage innocence to adult responsibility.

Daisy felt like a failure. She should have somehow been able to protect Zoe from all this. She should have shielded her better. "I'm sorry, Zo."

Zoe twisted the dish towel tighter, her knuckles shining white. "But what do I tell Daddy when he asks for Mom?"

A lump wedged itself in Daisy's throat. "The truth, I suppose."

"But the truth makes him cry." Zoe looked up, caught her sister's eye, her lips trembling with emotion she could barely suppress. Her expression was pleading, the lavender-blue depths filled with an agony that neither knew how to deal with. "Daddy's never going to get any better, is he?"

Daisy stood and headed for the stairs without answering Zoe's question. She couldn't answer. She didn't need to anyway. They both already knew the answer.

He should let her off. Nearly half a million dollars! It wasn't that much money, at least not now that he'd restored the Galván fortunes. But if he let her off, his adversaries would know and would broadcast his weakness. They were sniffing for his Achilles' heel, certain that sooner or later they'd expose it.

They probably would, too, he thought with a sigh, changing hands on the phone as he paced his hotel suite.

First there were problems with the Zimco acquisition, and now trouble was brewing with his young half sister, seventeen-year-old Anabella.

It had not been a good day so far and it was about to get much worse because he was forced to deal with his stepmother who couldn't roll out of bed without at least one or two good stiff drinks. It was now almost noon in Argentina, which meant Marquita must be halfway through a liter of vodka by now.

If he didn't care it would be so much easier. He could walk from his family, walk from the unbelievable debt his late father had left them, walk away from all of it and just do what he pleased.

Unfortunately, what pleased him was knowing he wasn't like his father. What pleased him was providing for his younger sisters. What pleased him was proving that he was as unlike his father as possible.

The screech of Marquita's voice in his ear brought him back to the moment. The phone dangled from his fingers as he paced the floor of his suite. Marquita was drunker than usual for noon. She must have finished her liter and started on a new bottle already.

"What's Anabella done now?" he asked with exaggerated patience.

Countess Marquita Galván immediately launched into an incoherent diatribe, gibberish words about Anabella and boys and running away from school.

Dante closed his eyes and drew a slow, deep breath. "Where is she?"

"At school, of course. She can't come here."

"Why not?" he asked. "She is your daughter."

"Because I can't deal with her. I can't handle her problems. I have problems of my own."

Yes, liquor, laziness, extravagance. His jaw hardened, a muscle popping close to his ear as he fought to contain his anger. Why had his stepmother ever had children? How could she have three and then abdicate all responsibility?

He suddenly pictured Tadeo, the lost one, the half brother who'd never made it to eighteen. Dante's heart felt wrenched. It actually felt broken in places. Would he never get over Tadeo's death? Would he ever be able to think of Tadeo without wanting to scream?

Tadeo was a great kid. Smart, funny, compassionate, sensitive. Sensitive. And it had killed him.

Dante was damned if he'd let Marquita's indifference destroy Anabella, too. "I'll be back in a couple days. Leave Anabella to me. I'll call the headmistress. I'll work this out."

"Thank goodness," Marquita breathed with relief. "I have a massage at two. I'd hate to miss that."

"That'd be a real tragedy."

Dante hung up, paced the suite another half dozen times before hesitating in front of the mirror hanging over the fireplace mantel.

Dark hair, light eyes, wide mouth. But he didn't see himself. He saw his father. Dante looked just like his father. It was a curse, he thought, a curse because he was constantly reminded that his father had not only failed him, but had failed all of them—his father had brought them all to the brink of destruction and abandoned them there.

Dante felt his father's sins again. Dante had saved the Galván family corporation from disaster, turned the bleak financial picture around, but that success meant nothing if he couldn't save Anabella.

And he couldn't do that here. He had to get back to Buenos Aires, which meant straightening out this mess with the Collingsworths and closing the door on what had been a very bad business deal.

Resolved on action, Dante picked up the phone, looked up the Collingsworth phone number, then punched in the seven digits. A soft voice answered on the second ring.

"Daisy Collingsworth?" he said sharply. He didn't want to be harsh, but he didn't like what he was going to do. He didn't want to nail the Collingsworths to the wall, but he couldn't afford to waste more time here. He needed to get on a plane. Needed to return home. One had to be tough to survive, he thought cynically. One had to take no prisoners.

"This is Zoe. Did you want Daisy?"

Zoe. Her voice was so gentle, almost tender, and he realized she couldn't be much older than Anabella.

His gut burned. His chest tightened. He felt like hell. "Yes. Is she available?"

He waited a good several minutes before someone picked up the phone. "This is Daisy."

Daisy's voice was firmer than Zoe's, a little huskier but no less feminine, and Dante suddenly pictured Daisy as she'd faced him at the track—pink T-shirt outlining full breasts, long legs sheathed in tight denim and the barest, softest lips he'd ever seen.

She was tall, blond and beautiful. And while her blue eyes looked cool, he'd seen enough of her temper to know she burned fire.

"Dante Galván here," he said, and then almost smiled when he heard her swift inhale. "It's time to get serious, *muneca.*"

CHAPTER TWO

HE WAS already at the track office when she pulled into the driveway. As she slammed the truck door shut behind her, Daisy caught a glimpse of Count Galván through the office window, and her stomach did a sudden wild free fall.

Perhaps her father had liked working with the Galváns, but she didn't. It wasn't just the issue of the stud fee. It wasn't an issue of trust, as much as one of personal dislike. The Galváns weren't known for their ethics, and Daisy despised anyone who took advantage of the weak. But that's how Dante's father had operated. Tino Galván preyed on struggling businesses, pumped them up with cash or promises of financial assistance and then later moved in for the kill, seizing not just the investment but the small business itself.

Dante was sitting on the edge of her desk reading a stack of paperwork when she walked through the door. She recognized the papers as their yearly farm report, a dismal record of all the losses they'd incurred in the last year. She couldn't help shuddering inwardly, recalling that disastrous fire. The losses had been horrifying. On paper the farm was an absolute disaster. But she refused to let him see her fear. ''Found what you wanted?'' she asked grimly.

He made a rough sound and gave his head a silent, derisive shake. "It's worse than I thought."

Daisy felt heat sweep through her, embarrassment and shame. "It's been a hard year."

"That's putting it mildly." He tossed the report onto the desk next to him, the paper sliding to a far corner. "You don't have any income. What happened to your great new breeding program? Where are your boarders? Your investors?"

She hated that she had to defend their business, especially to him, and still found it inconceivable that they owed his family so much money.

Nearly half a million dollars for a stud fee? Highway robbery, that's what it was. Daisy couldn't hide her hostility. "We have plenty of boarders. We're training more horses today than ever before."

"Pet ponies, not thoroughbreds."

"Our work may appear trivial to you, but we're a respected farm—"

"Without a competent manager," he softly interrupted.

"I *am* the manager."

"My point, exactly."

The gloves were off. He wasn't worried about hurting feelings any longer, or bloodying noses. It was war, and he intended to win.

He pushed off the desk and moved to the window. His narrowed gaze swept the distant farm buildings, focusing on the old barn in need of a new roof and the new stable, erected after the old one had burned down, that had yet to be painted. "You haven't paid me, and you certainly haven't maintained the farm. So what have you done with your money? How did you blow my father's investment?''

His words were a relentless assault, a hard pummeling that made her ache.

Daisy closed her eyes, swayed on her feet and wished for the first time in years that she'd never fallen in love with horses and hay and Collingsworth's green meadows.

She wished she didn't care so much about colts, yearlings and winning the big races. If she didn't care she could walk away from it all. If she didn't love the whole business so much she could give up on the disaster taking place at Collingsworth's and become someone else. But she did love the business—she loved the horses, the foals, the stallions, all of it.

He'd turned from the window and was studying her with the same detached scrutiny he'd viewed the farm buildings. Daisy felt his gaze all the way through her and dug her nails into her palms as heat flooded her middle. She didn't want to feel him. Didn't want to be aware of him. She wanted nothing to do with him. Not now. Not ever.

''We didn't blow that investment,'' she answered hotly, moved by emotions she couldn't name. Her heart raced as though she were one of the yearlings on the track, and she felt dangerously close to tears. ''Our farm has been struggling for a number of years. American farmers have been struggling for a decade. But we've made progress this year. We've made progress under my management.''

Her gaze met his as she emphasized the last words, her chin lifting defiantly. "I realize being Latin, and male, you don't want to work with a woman. But in this case, you don't have a choice. My father retired earlier this year. I run the farm now. I cut the checks. I make the decisions."

Dante turned completely around. "I have no problem working with women. I just don't like working with stupid people." He paused as her lips parted, her eyes widening. "But I don't think you're stupid. I think you're very intelligent and perceptive enough to realize I don't play games."

His arrogance made her see red, and yet beyond the emotional reaction came another response. Unwilling admiration. He'd dealt with conflict before. He was handling her like a pro.

It crossed her mind for the first time that she just might be in over her head.

What if she couldn't pull this off? What would happen to the farm and her family? She pictured Zoe, pictured her sister twisting and untwisting the dish towel.

A lump lodged in her throat, and she swallowed with difficulty. "I don't play games, either, Count Galván. I want nothing more than to work this out with you. But I have to be honest. I'm not prepared to lose the farm. It's been in our family since nineteen-eighteen, when my great-grandfather emigrated from Ireland. This is home."

"Miss Collingsworth—"

"No. Don't do it. Please. Give me one more year."

She saw a flicker of emotion in his face, his eyes

darkening and his jaw tensing. She felt his ambivalence and thought for a moment he'd relent. But then he gave his head a sharp shake.

"And do what?" He laughed shortly, "Watch as your barn burns down next? Sorry, *muneca*, can't do it."

She felt as though the air were being strangled from her. "Can't, or won't?"

"Both."

He did pity them, she thought faintly, it was there in his face, in his voice, in the cynical twist of his lips. His smile was bitter, the lower lip curling, accenting his high carved cheekbones and the hollows beneath.

My, he was beautiful, like a fallen angel, but only worse because he was real. Daisy had never felt so out of her depth before. How on earth was she supposed to pull this off? "Why not?" she whispered.

"Bad business. You make an exception for one, you've set a precedent. Before long you're making exceptions for all. So I don't do it. Won't do it. For anyone."

A soft, strangled sound ripped from her throat. She hadn't meant to cry out. She'd thought she had better control over herself.

She turned away, leaned against the desk, palms pressed flat on the scratched surface. She pressed hard, pressing against the suffocating desperation. It couldn't be this bad. It couldn't be the end. Everything was here. Her whole life was here. Even her mother was buried here.

Her rage threatened to boil over. "If your father were alive—"

"Your father shouldn't have agreed to work with him," he interrupted.

"My dad was charmed by your father." She dug her nails into the desk. "Charmed right out of the farm."

Dante saw her fingers whiten as she pressed them against the desk. Her blue eyes shone dark with pain, and her soft lips twisted, compressing to keep her misery within. She didn't want to reveal her suffering but she couldn't quite hide it.

This was his father's responsibility, and now it had become his.

He drew a slow breath, feeling the tightness in his chest, conscious of his self-disgust. His father, Tino, should never have made the deal with Bill Collingsworth. But his father had never been able to resist easy money, or what he perceived to be easy money. Tino had intended to take possession of Collingsworth Farm and add it to the stockpile of farms, ranches and family businesses that he was accumulating around the world.

The problem with Tino's plan had been that most of these family businesses were bankrupt or nearly bankrupt, and all were in need of massive infusions of cash.

Tino's greed had almost bankrupted Galván Enterprises and it had taken Dante nearly two years to break up and sell off two dozen debt-ridden ventures.

What a waste of time.

He'd arrived in Lexington to settle with the Collingsworths. The unpaid stud fee was the last debt uncollected, the last of the headaches Tino had left behind, and Dante needed closure. He needed to move forward and close the door on the past, but suddenly it wasn't that simple.

He rubbed the back of his neck, easing the knot of tension tightening the muscles there. He didn't owe the Collingsworths anything and didn't have to work with them, but Daisy was complicating everything.

Her golden blond beauty and leggy elegance had nothing to do with his change of heart. It was her courage, her intelligence, her passion for the horses.

He couldn't forget her expression as she watched the horses race earlier in the morning. He'd seen the wonder in her eyes and sensed her devotion. She loved the horses profoundly. It seemed criminal to make her suffer for her father's mistakes—and his.

Don't do it, he told himself. *Don't turn soft now. This is exactly why you and Father always fought. This is why he called you names.*

He swallowed, and his mouth tasted sour. This bad day was getting worse. Yet he couldn't ignore his conscience, couldn't throw the Collingsworths from their home.

If only he didn't feel so much, care so much, he might be a bigger success. He might be a multibillionaire instead of just a multimillionaire.

His lips twisted cynically. "Maybe there is a way," he said, pushing aside his personal fatigue to focus on the Collingsworths' needs.

He moved toward her, felt her stiffen as he leaned past her slender body to pick up the farm records. Heat surged through him as his arm brushed her shoulder. He hadn't meant to touch her, yet the touch felt electric.

Daisy slid from beneath his arm and moved quickly to the water cooler. She lifted a chipped cup from the shelf behind her but didn't fill it. Instead she stared at him, hands clasping the mug, apprehension in her eyes.

She'd felt the electricity, too, he thought. She'd felt the same current that had passed through him.

"What?" Her voice was pitched an octave lower.

She was right to be mistrustful. Dante's mouth tugged. His motives weren't entirely pure. He did want her more than he'd wanted any woman in a long, long time. "Let's look at the books together. Perhaps we've overlooked something."

Hands jerky, she filled her cup with water and brought it to her mouth, but she didn't drink. "When?"

"Now. Unless you have something more pressing to do?"

Three hours later Daisy wished she'd had something more pressing to do. She would have been willing to agree to Chinese water torture instead of looking at the farm books with Count Galván.

Three hours of shoulder-to-shoulder contact. Three hours of her thigh accidentally brushing his. Three hours of the most crazy tension imaginable, a tension that balled in her belly, tight and hard and heavy.

She wasn't attracted to him, was she?

Disconcerted, Daisy frantically pushed up and away from the desk, needing to create some immediate distance. She walked to the water cooler again and filled her cup, gulped the chilled water until it was gone.

"Are you all right?"

"Yes." *No.* She drew a small, shallow breath. The

truth was her head swam, her nerves were shot, and she felt terrible.

They'd come to no resolution about the debt, but one thing she knew. Dante Galván was not good for her. He made her feel nervous and unsure of herself and completely unbalanced. This wasn't the way she liked to function. This wasn't a comfortable sensation. It was making her sick.

"Should we take a break?" she suggested, thinking she definitely needed some air.

His dark gaze met hers and held. He searched her eyes. She didn't know what he was looking for and she certainly wasn't about to reveal anything more. She'd already exposed too much weakness.

"I think it's best if we just continue," he answered. "The sooner we get this settled, the sooner we can put this behind us."

Her wish exactly, she thought with a ragged sigh.

Finally, an hour later, they finished going through the records. They'd gone over every entry, discussed every line, checked her numbers.

Dante closed the report and sat back, stretching his legs in front of him. "How were you going to pull this off, Daisy?"

It was the second time today he'd called her by her given name, and the way he said her name undid her. He made her feel hot, awkward, self-conscious. She'd never felt uncomfortable in her skin before, but he was peeling away a protective layer and exposing raw nerves, tender nerves. How could he do this to her? How could he make her feel so—so…naked?

Feeling oddly undone, Daisy gathered the loose papers on her desk, the bills that he'd asked to see, the pedigrees on the new foals. She struggled to organize her thoughts even as her hands shuffled the paperwork. "I don't know, but I would have. I could have. I always do what I say I will."

"Always?"

Something in his voice made the air catch in her throat, and she looked at him, hands stilling, heart stopping. His dark gaze held hers.

He didn't believe her. But then he didn't know her determination or her sheer will. If she set her mind to something, she succeeded. Without a doubt. "I haven't broken my word yet."

He didn't say anything. He just kept looking at her, looking into her, and it was then she realized his eyes weren't dark brown. They were considerably lighter, almost the color of toffee ringed by a darker gold. What made his eyes appear dark was the intensity in his expression. His eyes were beautiful. Like the rest of him.

She felt heat rise through her, wave after wave of warmth until her cheeks burned and her lips felt as though they were melting.

"You're so sure of yourself," he said softly.

Her mouth tasted like sawdust. "I have to be." Was that her voice? "I love my home. If I can't find a way to keep the farm, then I've failed my family."

"But you didn't create this mess."

He was doing something to her, taking hold of some emotion inside her chest and shaping it, changing it, making it his. She didn't like it but she didn't know how to stop it.

Daisy rose to her feet. "It doesn't matter. It's my job to straighten it out."

He suddenly reached out and caught her hand in his, stopping her from moving away. "One person can only do so much. You're a smart woman, a strong woman, but you're just one person. This, *muneca*, is a huge farm. Right now you're understaffed, overworked and hip deep in red ink. Daisy, beyond the debt you owe to my family, what are you going to do?"

His fingers slipped to encircle her wrist. The pad of his thumb stroked her racing pulse. She felt as though she were melting, starting on the inside, deep down in her belly. The heat spread, as did the honey warmth, everywhere, making her aware of her thighs, her breasts, her oversensitized skin.

Her cheekbones felt scalding hot. She stared at him in mute fascination. His lips were perfectly shaped, his chin hard, a hint of a beard shadowing his jaw. She swallowed.

"Daisy?"

Her gaze lifted, and her eyes met his again. She wanted to kiss him. She wanted to know what his mouth would feel like. Wanted to know what a mouth like that could do.

"Daisy."

His voice was impossibly deep, increasingly husky. Even his accent sounded thicker, and she shivered inwardly, fearful and yet thrilled.

He tugged gently on her wrist, drawing her forward.

She sucked in air, her head feeling far too light. She couldn't remember when she'd last felt this way. If she'd ever felt this way. A kiss was just a kiss, but she wanted this kiss badly.

Yet just before his lips brushed hers, he hesitated, and his hesitation brought her firmly back to reality.

Was this any way to do business? Is this how she hoped to save Collingsworth Farm?

She must be out of her mind.

Daisy broke free and walked on wobbly legs to the far end of the office. She moved the window blind aside. The sun came through the glass in faded golden rays, highlighting a dust spiral in the middle of the floor.

"Now you know where the money's gone," she said, voice shaky, more breathless than usual.

He hadn't moved. He still sat in the leather chair at her desk. "Not exactly."

She looked at him over her shoulder. Her eyes met his. It was like touching a live wire. Every glance, every touch was a jolt, and the intensity of the jolts was making her tremble from head to toe. "What do you mean?"

"I don't understand about the stable. Why isn't there any record on the insurance settlement from the fire? Is there a reason you've kept it off the book?"

They'd kept nothing off the books. That would be illegal. Not to mention just plain wrong. "We don't operate that way," she answered flatly, wondering how he could say such things. Did he really think so little of them?

She drew a rough breath, trying to ignore the turbulent beat of her heart, and turned to look at the stable. The

building was less than six months old, the siding un-
painted, the wood still fragrant.

"Then tell me about the fire."

No, he wasn't going to put her through the third de-
gree about the fire now, was he? Did he really have so
little trust? "The fire is private. It's nobody's business
but ours."

"Answer the question, Daisy."

"No."

"If you don't work with me, I can't work with you."

She spun on him, her hair slapping her shoulder,
hands on her hips. "There you go, throwing your weight
around. It must be wonderful having that kind of power.
But I'm not going to go there, Count Galván. I'm not
going to lay down and grovel just because you want to
feel superior."

His jaw tightened. "That's not why I'm asking."

"No? What is your point then?"

"The settlement on the stable would have been at
least a quarter million dollars. It would have gone a long
way to paying off your debt. But there's been no record
of a settlement in your books. Why?"

"Maybe because there's been no settlement."

"You haven't received a payout?"

"No."

"Nothing?"

She almost felt like laughing. It must be nerves. "Not
even a penny." She saw his incredulity. "We were in-
sured, but it's all tied up in litigation."

He didn't speak. He didn't have to. She could see
exactly what he was thinking. The rumors were every-

where—in Lexington, in the neighboring farms, at the track. It was whispered that the fire had been purposely set. The Collingsworths had risked cashing in on their bankrupt farm. They were trying to bail out of the business before they were chased out.

Nothing could be further from the truth.

But Count Galván didn't care about facts. He'd already formed his own opinion. She saw his horror, felt his disgust. No animal lover could imagine setting one's stables on fire to enjoy a fat insurance policy, but that was what everyone thought they'd done.

That was what Count Galván thought they'd done.

She left the window and crossed the floor to stand within a foot of him. "The rumors are false."

"The fire wasn't deliberately set?"

She'd never forget that night, the heat, the dense, suffocating smoke, the acrid smell. She'd never seen anything like it in her life. The flames had been ungodly. The stable went up in minutes. No time for the fire department to come, no time for anything.

When it looked as though they'd lose the mares still trapped in the stalls, grizzled old Teddy McCaw, their thirty-year-veteran trainer, dashed into the inferno and saved the terrified horses. But he wasn't able to save himself.

Daisy's eyes burned, her throat thickening with a grief she couldn't share. "Who on earth would do such a thing? Me? My father? My sister? What kind of people do you think we are?"

"People in need of easy money."

Pure instinct, instinct and fury, drove her fist. She

swung at him and connected with his jaw. She didn't even feel the pain in her hand, fury and pain blinding her. "Go to hell!"

He caught her wrist in his hand, imprisoning it, his fingers hard around the slender bones. "That's not going to get you anywhere."

She tried to ignore the burst of heat surging through her middle, his touch both painful and electric. "I don't want to get anywhere with you, Count Galván. I resent your questions, and I resent the implications. I don't know what kind of people you do business with, but we're not like them. The Collingsworths are a family business, run by family. Now let me go."

"Don't take another swing."

"I won't. I don't need any broken bones."

He let her go, and she cradled her hand against her chest. Her fingers hurt. The knuckles, bones and joints throbbed. It felt like she'd slammed her hand into a brick wall.

No wonder she hadn't punched anyone since hitting Tommy Wilcox all those years ago. It hurt throwing punches.

But if she was going to hit anyone, she was glad she hit Dante. He deserved it. She felt absolutely no remorse.

Daisy swore beneath her breath and rubbed her sore hand and wrist.

"Hurt?" he managed to drawl the word without sounding the least bit sympathetic.

Her eyes snapped fire and fury. "No."

"Did you damage anything? It sounded like eggshells breaking."

"Those were just the cobwebs in your brain."

His eyes glinted. He seemed amused. "You don't know when to stop, do you?"

"Get out."

"I don't think so." Without asking permission, he took her hand in his and ran his thumb over her throbbing knuckles. Her fingers had begun to swell. But worse than the pain in her knuckles were the crazy sensations in her belly.

Every place he touched tingled. It was warfare on her senses. Her hand felt sensitive, and yet it was her body responding, her body quivering and melting and aching for things she'd never even cared about before.

When he looked at her, the mocking smile was still there in his toffee-colored eyes. "You're right. Nothing's broken. But you do need ice. It's already starting to swell."

"I'll remember that."

"Tell me where you keep the ice."

"I'll do it when you're gone."

He muttered something inelegant. "Daisy, I'm not leaving until you've iced your hand. You're the only one running this farm. You have to be able to work tomorrow. So sit down, be quiet and stop fighting me."

"I'm not fighting you. You're fighting with me. You keep forgetting this is *my* farm."

He gazed at her, his expression half amused, half exasperated. "Are you always so stubborn?"

"Stubborn's not a bad thing, Count Galván. It just depends on the situation." She hated that he made her feel willful, like a child. "There's ice in the kitchen, in the little freezer. But I don't need your help."

He brought her a makeshift ice pack, ice cubes wrapped in a dish towel. "Yes, you do. You just don't know it yet."

Dante placed the ice bag on her hand. "You should never lose your temper like that. It's the fastest way to let the enemy take the upper hand."

"Your words, not mine." She hated that when he touched her she burned. She hated that his eyes made her feel things, want things. She hated that he had to be the reasonable one now, after he'd provoked her into losing her temper.

It was crazy, the way she felt, nerves shot full of adrenaline. It was the same rush she got when riding an unbroken horse—danger, fear, anticipation. But this was not the kind of reaction she wanted to have. Not to a man, and especially not to Dante Galván.

Daisy pressed the ice bag more firmly to her knuckles, trying to ignore the throbbing in her hand and the bittersweet ache in her chest. "I think we're finished."

He regarded her steadily, speculation in his hard gaze. And then he smiled. "Finished? No, Daisy, not by a long shot. We've got quite a bit of unfinished business between us still. But I do know a way to settle the debt. You have something I want."

"I do?"

"Kentucky Kiss."

The blood drained from her face. Her horse, her mare, her fifteenth birthday present? "Kentucky Kiss?"

CHAPTER THREE

DAISY struggled to her feet, the ice bag slipping crookedly off her arm. "Kentucky Kiss isn't for sale."

"She's a valuable dam."

"No." Her father had given her Kentucky Kiss when she turned fifteen, and for nearly two weeks after her birthday, Daisy had slept in the stable, snuggled in a sleeping bag inside the yearling's stall.

"Surely you've had offers." Dante persisted.

Daisy dropped the ice bag on the desk. "That's not the point. She's not for sale. Kentucky Kiss is the heart of Collingsworth Farm." And was her heart, too.

"Daisy, we should at least discuss this."

"I'll consider other horses. We have a dozen dams—"

"My interest is only in Kentucky Kiss. I know her pedigree. Four foals, three to race, two winners. She's the one I want. She's extremely valuable. If you sold her to me, you'd erase the debt."

Daisy couldn't speak. Words were impossible. She simply stood there, fingertips braced on the desk, heart beating so slowly she felt the weight of every second, the pressure building inside her until she felt like a balloon about to burst.

So much had been taken away from her. Her mother.

Teddy McCaw. Her father's health. Her college education.

And now her horse.

But Kentucky Kiss was more than a horse. She'd been Daisy's best friend. When Daisy groomed Kiss, she'd told her everything, confided everything, shared her secrets and her longing and her dreams. And maybe it sounded stupid, but Kentucky Kiss understood Daisy. Kentucky Kiss loved her, and accepted her, and just let her be herself.

Daisy took a shaky step toward the water cooler but then couldn't take another. Her legs were too weak. She couldn't move in either direction. "Kentucky Kiss is the heart of our breeding program."

"Yes, now she is, but her foal, Miracle Baby, will be your future."

She pictured Kentucky Kiss's foal, Miracle Baby, who'd just turned twelve weeks old and was still all gawky legs. She could see him tripping about behind his mother in coltish ecstasy.

If Miracle Baby went to auction as a yearling, it had already been speculated that he'd go for at least a million dollars, probably two to three times as much if in the next year he was raised by the right trainer, handled as a champion should be handled.

Daisy knew she needed to hire a big-name trainer for the foal, but she didn't have the money to do it. She wouldn't be able to attract a reputable trainer if the farm continued to hover on the verge of bankruptcy. Reputation meant everything in this business. And horse people were susperstitious. You had to have a good name. You had to have wins. And you needed luck.

Which was why Daisy had told no one about her father's illness. Collingsworth Farm would be finished if people knew her father was as sick as he was.

"We need a trainer," she said slowly, staring out the window and yet seeing nothing.

How could she sell Kentucky Kiss? But the farm had been in the family forever, and there was Zoe's future to think about. How could she *not* sell Kentucky Kiss? "You can have Kentucky Kiss for six hundred thousand. That will settle the debt and pay for a trainer for Miracle Baby."

"Six hundred?"

"And you leave her here until Miracle Baby is weaned."

He seemed to consider this. "You'll put this in writing?"

"I'll get the paperwork together later tonight. We can take it to a notary first thing tomorrow." At least she wouldn't have to part with Kentucky Kiss immediately. She'd have another four months. Six, if she was lucky.

And she did feel lucky, luckier than she had in a year. Keeping the farm was what mattered. Keeping her father in his own house. Keeping Zoe's inheritance intact.

Selling Kentucky Kiss was a personal sacrifice and maybe one her father wouldn't approve of, but she was doing it for the right reasons. She was doing it for the right people.

"I'll meet you tomorrow downtown," she said, naming a prominent law firm that handled transactions like this one. In Lexington, breeders and buyers left nothing to chance.

He waited outside as she locked up the office for the night. She didn't intend to return until morning. In the evenings Daisy liked to give Zoe a break from taking care of their dad. Earlier in the year Zoe used to drive into town to meet her old high school friends. They'd catch a movie, get coffee, just hang out together. But lately Zoe didn't go out anymore, and her friends didn't call that often, either.

Dante opened the truck door for Daisy. "Your hand is bothering you," he said.

"It aches," she admitted, knowing she only had herself to blame. Losing her temper was stupid. It just made her look immature.

"Take something when you get home. It'll help with the swelling."

"Right." Daisy slid behind the wheel, wanting nothing more than to escape. It was embarrassing having Dante worry about her bruised hand. She'd been the one to lose control. She'd thrown the punch.

But Dante held on to the green truck door, his foot resting on the old Chevy's riser. He studied her for a long minute, his expression impossible to read. "I have an invitation to the Lindleys' black-tie party tomorrow night," he said finally. "Would you consider going with me?"

"The Lindleys?" she repeated, wrapping one hand around the steering wheel, gripping the ridges tightly.

"It's the big horse event of the year."

Daisy knew all about the Lindleys' preauction party.

It was an annual event, and the funds raised went to charity. Last year it was literacy. This year a women's shelter. But this year, like last year, the Collingsworths hadn't been invited.

Her lips parted, but no sound came out. She struggled to put voice to words and still came up with nothing. Peter Lindley had been her father's best friend. Peter Lindley had dropped her father like a hot potato.

"I don't think so," she said at length, her voice a squeak, her throat so tight she couldn't say more. She didn't hate the Lindleys, but there was no love lost between the families.

But Dante didn't take no easily. "Why not?"

"We're not exactly popular people in Lexington."

"Then fake it."

He smiled, and she'd never seen him look more confident. "I...can't. I hate those things. I hate the snobbery, the superficial small talk, the absurd money the women spend on clothes. It's just not me."

"You're not a fashion darling, then?"

She felt herself blush. He was making fun of her. It was obvious she wasn't into high fashion. She lived in her boots and jeans. They were comfortable and practical. "No."

He reached out, touched her cheek gently. "You don't need designer clothes to make you stand out. You're beautiful, Daisy. You turn heads just as you are."

His fingers scorched her skin, and heat flooded her limbs. She drew a shaky breath and was suddenly grateful she was sitting down because she didn't think she'd have the strength to stand. "You don't need to flatter me, Count Galván. I can live without compliments."

His lips twisted. "We're past the formalities, Daisy. It's Dante now. It has to be. Once a woman hits me, there's no going back."

Heat surged through her. She felt herself blush yet again, the color staining higher, hotter beneath her skin. He was having the worst effect on her. "I don't know what to say."

"Say yes, say you'll go to the Lindleys' with me."

She looked up, and her eyes met his. His eyes were such a light toffee color, beautiful like topaz. Her heart did a strange double thump, two painful beats in one. She'd never survive an evening alone with him. She'd be tied up in knots. She'd wish for things she shouldn't ever wish for.

Like another touch from his hands.

She loved it when he brushed her cheek just now. She loved the tingle in her skin and the clench of her belly and the heat in her veins. She loved the powerful response as much as she loved the newness of it. It was the first good thing she'd felt in so long.

In years.

"No," she blurted. "I can't. I'm sorry, but I have obligations at home. It's Zoe's night out tomorrow."

He regarded her steadily. "Switch nights with her."

"It doesn't work that way."

"No?"

She felt like she was falling, tumbling forward into the warm gold-brown eyes, tumbling headfirst into emotion, and emotion was all wrong for her. Emotion meant trouble. "No," she whispered, her voice faint even to her own ears.

"Then I won't go, either."

"No—"

"Yes. If you won't go with me, I don't want to be there. It's you I want to be with. Not the Lindleys."

Looking at him, looking into his face she almost changed her mind. It would be amazing to go to the formal party on his arm. He'd look incredible in a tuxedo. He'd break every woman's heart.

Daisy swallowed, her throat dry as sandpaper. She needed to get out of here. She'd do something stupid soon. Say something stupid. Maybe say yes, maybe say kiss me, maybe say touch my cheek and make me feel beautiful again.

"I'll call you when I have the paperwork in order," she said, voice husky, heart thudding hard, too hard. She wanted to cry and she didn't even know why. Nothing was wrong. Everything was fine. Kentucky Kiss would get them out of debt, and life would go on.

"Okay." He smiled, and then he lifted a strand of silver-gold hair from her cheek and carefully tucked it behind her ear. "Call me when you're ready."

She sucked in air, her chest on fire. "I will."

But as she drove home, wincing with each shift of the transmission, she knew she'd never call him. She'd finish the business arrangements, and that would be the end.

Daisy was smart enough to know when she was in over her head, and with Dante, she was definitely in the deep end, woefully out of depth.

Reaching the drive leading to the house, Daisy changed gears yet again. The truck's old manual transmission required rigorous shifting, and each throw of the stick sent shooting pain through Daisy's right hand. *If you think you hurt now,* she told herself, *just imagine what it would be like to get involved with him. Don't do it. Keep your distance. Focus on the business.*

The sunlight was waning fast as Daisy entered the house. Warm gold light shone through the lacy dining room curtains and gilded the fading cabbage rose wallpaper. In the red-gold light the full-blown roses looked almost real. Daisy stopped to touch one dusty pink rose.

"Daddy never liked this wall paper."

It was Zoe. She'd entered the dining room behind Daisy. Daisy turned to look at her sister. "But it was Mom's wall paper. Mom picked it out before you were born."

"So Daddy never changed it."

"Dad never stopped loving Mom." Daisy's voice throbbed with emotions she rarely let surface. Dante had stirred something to life in her, and she was finding it difficult to stamp it back down.

Gently she traced the outline of a lavender rose. The blossom's edge curled like lettuce. Soft, wavy, delicate. But beneath those fragile petals lay sharp dark thorns.

Just like life.

Daisy faced Zoe. "I'm selling Kentucky Kiss. Count Galván is buying her for six hundred thousand."

"Daisy, you can't do that."

"We'll be able to afford some help for Dad now," she continued as though Zoe had never spoken. "I'll also look for a trainer to work with Miracle Baby. Miracle Baby is the answer. If he goes high at auction—"

"Daisy, you can't sell Kentucky Kiss."

Daisy felt like she'd swallowed a bucket of nails. "I'm all right with this."

"There's got to be another way."

"If we'd gotten the insurance settlement things might have been different, but..." Her shoulders lifted, fell. "But we didn't get it."

"We still might."

"Zoe, they think *we* set the fire. This will be tied up for years in court. We can't wait. If we keep bouncing checks, if we can't bring on another trainer, we're dead in the water."

Zoe shut her eyes and pressed her palms against her forehead. "This is bad," she whispered.

"It could be worse, though. We could have no options. We could be on the streets—"

"You can't sell Kentucky Kiss to Count Galván."

"Of course I can. She's my horse. It's my decision."

"Then get the count to wait a year. He has to wait."

"Dante's not going to wait. We've already made him wait for payment on the stud fee. He's done waiting."

"I don't think he has a choice," Zoe answered in a small voice. "I've promised Carter Scott he could breed his new stallion with Kentucky Kiss next year."

Carter Scott, a former customer who'd asked Daisy to marry him once. *"What?"*

Daisy rarely raised her voice. She didn't need to raise her voice, but she couldn't help it at the moment. She was shocked. Beyond shocked. "You've got to be kidding."

"I wish I was."

"Zoe, she's not your horse. You don't run the farm. You have no right to make arrangements for our best dam. What on earth would possess you to do such a thing?"

"Dad. I did it for Dad." Then she explained, hesitantly reminding Daisy about the new study the university hospital was doing on Alzheimer's.

Daisy had discovered the new treatment, one so controversial that health insurance wouldn't touch it. But despite her best efforts to raise more cash, including getting a second mortgage on the farm property, Daisy couldn't scrape up enough to allow him to participate.

It had been a devastating realization, and breaking the news to Zoe had been awful.

"I couldn't accept no," Zoe continued faintly. "I couldn't accept that he wouldn't get help because we didn't have enough money." Tears trembled on Zoe's lashes. "I couldn't let the opportunity slip away."

"You entered Dad in the hospital program?"

"Carter Scott gave me the money in advance for breeding his stallion with Kentucky Kiss. He'll own the foal, and he's agreed to pay all boarding and medical fees."

"How much money did he give you?"

"Two hundred and fifty thousand."

Daisy pressed her knuckles to the wallpaper. Two hundred and fifty thousand dollars? On top of the fee they already owed Dante?

The mountain of debt staggered Daisy. For a moment she couldn't think. She just knew she couldn't do this anymore. She couldn't keep juggling bills and problems and mistakes and keep it all together. It was too much. The stress of it was just too much.

She heard a strange low buzzing in her ears. Like static on a radio.

"I thought you'd be happy." Zoe's voice sounded strained. "I thought you'd be glad I found a solution."

Daisy struggled to focus. She looked at Zoe and realized Zoe wasn't doing very well, either. Her skin looked ashen. Her lavender-blue eyes were enormous. "I guess Dad is participating now in the hospital program?" she asked.

Zoe nodded. "He's on new medication. We go in to the hospital once a week for follow-up and blood tests."

Daisy didn't speak.

Zoe's hands clenched, nails digging into her fists. "I can't give up on him. I want him back. I want him the way he used to be."

Daisy's eyes burned. It would kill Zoe to watch their dad wither away, and it would happen before their eyes. His memory would go. His control would go. His mind...

She shook her head, not wanting to think that way. This was hard on her, but it would be doubly painful for Zoe. Daisy's sister had never got to know their mom, as she'd died just after Zoe was born. Now Zoe would lose Dad, too.

How could she blame Zoe for fighting for Dad? How could she blame her for loving him so much? "I'm glad you did it, Zo. I wish I'd done it." Her voice broke. "Somebody should try to save Dad."

It was a great sentiment, Daisy thought a half hour later as she stood on the farm house's front porch, but it didn't change the fact that they were now indebted to two people for three quarters of a million dollars. And that wasn't including interest.

It also meant she had to talk to Dante.

She knew he carried a cell phone but she didn't have that number so she phoned his hotel. He wasn't in. Daisy left a message for him to call, and then she remembered that he'd mentioned a business function this evening. He'd said he was meeting someone at the Derby Club for drinks before a dinner engagement.

Daisy glanced at her watch. If she hurried, she might still be able to catch him at the Derby.

The club exuded old-world comfort and class; the walls were paneled, the furniture all large sturdy pieces upholstered in butterscotch and burgundy leather. The club provided owners and breeders with a place to gather and discuss the subject they loved best—horses.

Daisy pushed through the entrance, ignoring the discreet, suit-and-tie employee trying desperately to wave her out. "Members only, miss," he said, stepping in front of her, his smile politely frigid.

"Yes," she said, smiling stiffly before sidestepping him and walking past. "I know." They used to be members. Back when they could afford luxuries.

Daisy ignored the proliferation of brass plaques mounted to the wall, plaques reading No Denim in Clubhouse, Members Only and Men Only in the Lounge.

She entered the library, her gaze roving the clusters of men and women. The suit-and-tie staff member who'd stopped Daisy at the door cornered her. "You can't be here. This is a private club."

"I need to see someone. I won't be long."

Members were watching. Even the smokers standing around the library's brandy cart paused to see what the commotion was about.

She felt a crackle of electricity, a new hum of tension. "What's the problem?" It was Dante.

Daisy swung around, feeling an inexplicable thrill at seeing him. She hadn't expected to feel a ripple of excitement, but he did something to her, made her pulse race. "I need to talk to you."

"Is she your guest, sir?" The club employee wasn't pleased.

"Yes."

"Denims aren't permitted in the clubhouse, sir."

"We'll talk outside, then." Dante placed a hand on her lower back.

He didn't push her or pressure her, and yet his touch made her tense, her spine shuddering at the razor sharp sensations rippling beneath her skin. All her nerve endings were alive and connected. She felt so much. She felt too much.

"I'm sorry about that," she said, referring to the awkward scene in the library.

"I've dealt with worse," he answered as they stepped outside onto the broad front porch. "So what's wrong? Something serious must have happened if you chased me down here."

Daisy turned her back on the views of darkened, endless emerald-green pastures. The air smelled ripe and fresh, a welcome change after the club's smoky interior. She might as well get this over with. "We'll have to put off signing the sale papers tomorrow. There seems to be a small problem with some of the documents."

"You've changed your mind."

His tone sounded ominously flat. She suddenly sensed he'd be ruthless in negotiations and realized she didn't want him as an adversary. "No," she denied swiftly. "It's not that at all."

"Then what is it?"

"Just details."

His narrowed gaze swept her face, searching for a sign of deception. "You're not shopping her around, are you?"

"*No*. I promise."

Tension emanated from him in waves. His jaw jutted, and grooves formed on either side of his mouth. "Because I won't pay more, Daisy, and I won't jump through hoops. We made a deal. I expect you to honor it."

"Just as I intend to honor it," she answered tightly.

His jaw eased. "Good." He was smiling again. "When I saw you in the library I hoped you were here because you'd changed your mind about going to the Lindleys' tomorrow night. You haven't, have you?"

"No. I'm sorry."

His smile was one of pure regret. "No, *I'm* sorry."

*   *   *

Later that night, at home in bed, Daisy lay on her back and stared at the ceiling. The roof sloped above her head and the dormer window let in moonlight. The trees outside patterned her ceiling with the outline of leaves, and it was like a mosaic, she thought, the texture and shape of leaves and branches against the white paint.

Dante wasn't going to let her off the hook. He wanted Kentucky Kiss and he didn't want to be jerked around over the purchase. She didn't blame him. He'd been jerked around enough by her family.

So if Dante wouldn't back down, it meant Carter Scott would have to.

Daisy closed her eyes. She dreaded going to see Carter Scott, but that's what she'd do, first thing tomorrow.

But the next morning the truck had a flat tire, and one of the stable hands never showed up for work, so Daisy tackled his feeding and grooming chores after painfully jacking up the truck to get the tire changed.

Lunch was a rushed affair at the house, and there were phone calls to return and more stable chores to finish before she could finally break away to see Carter.

It was quarter to four when she climbed in her truck. Carter Scott lived on a wide residential boulevard in an exclusive Lexington neighborhood where the houses looked remarkably alike and were blueprints for the classic Southern mansion—brick steps, stately white columns and wrought-iron gates.

Her truck sputtered as she parked in the circular driveway, and as she rang the doorbell she noticed the dust on her boots and the grime on her jeans. She was filthy. This wasn't exactly the right approach to take with

Carter. He appreciated fine things. He would have appreciated Daisy more if she were…clean.

Carter's housekeeper ushered Daisy to the formal high-ceilinged parlor at the front of the house, and Carter appeared almost immediately. He greeted Daisy warmly, offered her iced tea, which Daisy declined, and then something stronger, which Daisy also declined.

Five minutes of small talk was the best she could stomach. At the first conversational lull, Daisy brought up the problem. "Carter, something's happened that shouldn't have happened, and I need your help."

"Anything, Daisy. You know how I feel about you."

"Yes," she hurriedly continued, trying not to squirm. All of Lexington had dumped them, all, that is, but Mr. Scott. He'd seized on the Collingsworths' bad fortune as an opportunity to get a young bride at an elegant price. At least that's the way Daisy saw it. "I understand you made Zoe a very generous loan."

"It wasn't a loan. It was payment on a contract."

"Unfortunately, it's a contract I can't honor."

"The contract's legal, Daisy."

"Carter, you know you can't go to Zoe on farm matters. I manage the farm."

"But this was between your dad and me. Zoe was just acting as his power of attorney." Carter shifted in his chair and crossed one leg over the other. He'd once been blond but was quickly turning gray. Even his long handlebar moustache was graying. "Your sister does have that right, doesn't she?"

"Yes."

"We met at Pembroke, Pembroke and Brown, the law

firm that represents your family. Everything was done in accordance with your father's wishes."

But my father didn't know what he was doing. Or did he? Daisy needed an aspirin badly. "I've sold Kentucky Kiss. She's not mine to breed."

His expression didn't change. "My contract with Collingsworth Farm supercedes any other arrangement you've made for Kentucky Kiss."

"Carter, please."

He didn't answer. His gaze dropped, and he stared into his crystal tumbler and wrinkled his nose before taking another long drink. "Go with me to the Lindleys' tonight and I'll think about it."

"Oh, Carter—"

He didn't plead, didn't protest, he just waited. She couldn't believe he'd do this, but what did she expect? Other people's vulnerabilities made Carter feel strong. "You're not being fair," she said at length.

"No, you're not being fair. You know how I feel about you. You want something from me. Why shouldn't I want something from you?" He must have noticed her stunned expression because he hurriedly added, "Not that, Daisy. I'm a gentleman."

"Carter, you're a friend and a nice man but I don't love you, and I can't marry someone I don't love."

"You've never given me a chance."

Daisy looked at him and felt the hopelessness of her situation. She knew she'd already told Dante no about the party and it seemed wrong—no, it *was* wrong—to accept a date from Carter. But did she have a choice?

"If I go with you, you'll consider tearing up the contract?"

"I'll consider it."

"And what would it take for you to actually do it?" She couldn't believe she put the question to him, but she might as well have it out in the open. If he wanted to barter, she needed to know what was on the table.

He swigged the rest of his whiskey. "I don't think we need to go there...yet."

Daisy had her answer. He'd break the contract if she married him.

CHAPTER FOUR

DAISY gazed at her reflection in the mirror, dazzled by the shimmer of silver sequins, glitter drop earrings and the elegant upswept hairdo.

If she didn't know herself, she'd think the sparkling blonde lived a glamorous life on the social circuit far from farm life. But since it was her, she knew exactly what she was seeing—fake diamond earrings, a cheap sequin top and Zoe's white taffeta skirt left over from her debutante party two years ago.

Was she out of her mind? Was she really going to the Lindleys' preauction party with Carter Scott dressed like this?

She looked like Carter's dream date, she told her reflection morosely. Ugh. A fate worse than death.

Knots formed in her shoulders, and distaste rippled through her middle. She couldn't believe Carter was making her play this game. She couldn't believe she was agreeing to it.

The only one she really wanted to see tonight was Dante. And he wouldn't even be at the party.

Thank goodness.

Tentatively Daisy touched the waist of her long white taffeta skirt, the skirt full with layers of stiff petticoats. The skirt would pass, but her top's silver spangles practically blinded her. As she looked up, blue eyes mirrored her uncertainty, and she felt a tremor of trepidation.

The Lindleys were not going to welcome her with open arms. The Lindleys might even try to embarrass her.

She closed her eyes, found her courage and a little of her old backbone. If she was going to go through with this, then she'd do it her way. She couldn't be fake. The Collingsworths were good people. They didn't have to put on airs.

Carefully using her bruised hand, Daisy unpinned the coil of hair, and the long pale mass came tumbling down, falling past her shoulder blades to the middle of her back. Stick-straight hair, the blond of flax, the texture of corn silk. Next she wiped off most of the lipstick, reducing the fuchsia stain to a soft pink. There, at least she looked more real.

So real that when she gazed into the mirror she saw herself as a little girl, perched on the bathroom counter watching her father adjust his black bow tie. She could see him wink at her in the mirror, creases fanning from his cornflower-blue eyes, still so young and movie star handsome. Her father was amazing. He'd been a wonderful father.

He still was.

The bathroom door opened and Zoe popped her head in. "Mr. Scott's here," Zoe said. Then she caught sight of her sister. "Daisy. You look…you look beautiful."

"No."

"Yes. You look like Mom."

Daisy's eyes welled with tears, and she looked at the

ceiling, stared at the bubble-dome light fixture and counted to ten, counted to keep the tears from blinding her and ruining her mascara. "Mom was so much prettier than me," she said, voice husky. "Mom was Miss Texas."

"You look like Miss Texas."

"Stop, Zoe. You're going to ruin my makeup."

Her sister laughed, and then they were hugging. "Have fun, Daisy. Show Lexington we're still the best."

Carter smiled his approval when Daisy descended the stairs. "I wish you'd wear dresses more often," he said as he escorted her to his car, a big black Rolls-Royce. "You look like a real lady in dresses."

She smiled tightly. "Thank you." But she didn't want dresses and the life of a Southern lady.

"I could make you happy, Daisy."

Already he was referring to a life together. She knew it would happen but hadn't expected the pressure to start so early. "Let's just enjoy the party, okay?"

Ten minutes later they were turning off the main road, heading down the Lindleys' private drive. Through the thicket of trees Daisy could see the white canvas party tents dotting the endless manicured lawn, the enormous tents shimmering with light.

Daisy had expected gawking. She'd expected a few scandalized whispers, but not the turn of every head as she and Carter made their appearance. People were staring. Everyone was staring. Openly.

Even for Daisy it was tough to bear. Yet when the whispers reached her ears, whispers about her father and speculation that they'd lost everything because he was a drunk and a gambler, she found her spine and her strength. Instead of cowering she grew taller, lifted her chin higher. She refused to crawl beneath a rock and hide. They didn't know the first thing about the Collingsworths.

They moved through the crowded ballroom to the stone terrace at the back of the house. From the terrace there was another flight of stairs to the party tents on the lawn.

The moon was high, and the evening felt warm. It was a perfect night for a party.

"A drink?" Carter asked, placing his hand on her arm.

"Please."

"Cocktail or wine?"

Daisy forced a smile, even as she wished he'd take his hand off her arm. She didn't dislike Carter but she didn't welcome his touch. "Anything."

"All right, wait here," he said, bringing her hand to his mouth and kissing the back of it.

He left her at the balustrade. Daisy stood at the low stone wall and gazed down on the lawn. Throngs of partygoers moved below. Tuxedos surrounded by glistening ruby, gold, sapphire gowns. The fabrics of the gowns were equally luxurious, dresses made of silk, chiffon and velvet. The ladies shone like exotic jewels next to the men in their formal black tie.

Leaning forward, she watched one man make his way through the crowd. He was tall, taller than the rest, and very broad through the shoulders. She couldn't see his face, but something deep inside her turned inside out.

Dante Galván.

He was walking slowly, greeting people now and again, shaking hands with one older gentleman before acknowledging another.

Even from the terrace he looked too tall, too strong, too imposing. He didn't creep through life, she thought faintly. He dominated it, dictated it, drove it.

How long she watched him, she didn't know, but then slowly he turned, and as if aware of her, looked up. His gaze immediately riveted on her.

Her breath suddenly caught in her throat. She'd thought all men looked handsome in tuxedos, but Dante Galván defined one. The black silk tie set off his Roman nose and chin, the white shirt played up the bronze in his coloring and the elegant cut of the jacket gave him old-world glamour.

He was beautiful. Too beautiful.

His gaze seemed to embrace her. He was taking her in, studying every detail, from the strands of her loose silvery blond hair to the tips of her white satin heels, before inching up to rest on her silver sequin halter top with its plunging décolleté and skimpy coverage.

She was sure he could see beneath the flimsy fabric, was sure he was aware she'd gone braless. A peculiar curl of warmth centered in her belly, extending in bright tingling rays, heating her skin, gathering in her breasts and creating an ache deep within her pelvis.

She'd never felt such an intense physical response before—and all he'd done was *look* at her.

Daisy couldn't move. Dante remained at the bottom

of the staircase. She wanted him to climb the stairs, join her on the terrace, but he waited where he was.

Nervously she took a step down the marble stairs and then hesitated, nerves on edge. He wasn't saying anything. He wasn't moving. He was simply waiting for her.

She was nearing the bottom of the stairs. Her legs felt like Jell-O, but suddenly she didn't think she could take another step. "Won't you say anything?" Her voice sounded strangled.

"What do you want me to say?"

"Whatever you're thinking."

"Really?"

"Might as well tell me what's on your mind. I know you asked me here tonight, and yet here I am with someone else—"

"I've been rejected before." He was smiling faintly and his expression was wry.

"It wasn't like that."

"Do I dare ask about Kentucky Kiss?"

Her throat sealed closed. Heat burned across her cheekbones. "No," she whispered.

"I see." He cocked his head, studied her intently, his gaze so hard and real it was almost a physical thing. "That doesn't leave us much to talk about."

Daisy's heart fell, plummeting to her stomach and then all the way down. She couldn't explain it, couldn't justify the disappointment, it just was. "You're angry."

"No. I'm curious, and a little surprised, but definitely not angry. How could I be angry with you? You look—" and his mouth twisted into a lazy, sinful smile "—incredible. Good enough to eat."

* * *

It was true, Dante thought, as she took a step closer. She was putting ideas in his head, making him want to try things he was quite sure she'd never done before.

He watched her descend the rest of the staircase, focused on the swing of her hips, the shape of her legs, the slight bounce of her breasts. He'd bet a thousand dollars she wasn't wearing a bra, and it made him ache to touch her, to slide his hands up her back, around her rib cage and cup her breasts. He wanted to feel her body, her skin, her incredibly lush curves.

"I'm here with an old family friend."

"Carter Scott. Yes, I know him." Dante couldn't keep the contempt from his voice. "What does he want from you now?"

Daisy's head jerked up. "How do you know? What do you mean?"

"The last time your father and my father talked, apparently your father mentioned that Carter had proposed. Your father was against it."

"My father lets me make my own decisions."

Dante glanced at her sleek fair head, her long silvery hair hanging straight to the dip in her back, the pale strands brushing the shimmering sequins at her narrow waist. "Has he proposed again?"

She drew herself back, blue eyes flashing with indignation. "That's really none of your business."

Her lips were the fullest, softest pink he'd ever seen. "He's too old for you, Daisy."

"He can't be much older than you!" She flashed the words back.

He smiled and realized he'd found another American rebel.

The first American rebel hadn't even been his, but one of his father's girlfriends. Dante was ten when he met the first of his father's many girlfriends, bumping into the beautiful blond American by the side of an exclusive Buenos Aires hotel swimming pool.

Kate was her name, short for Kathleen Lyons, heir to the United States East Coast Lyons chemical and plastic fortune. Smart, funny, breezy, Kate wasn't impressed by the Galván money—she just loved being around Tino.

Kate didn't last. None of the girlfriends lasted. Although eventually Dante met many other girlfriends, he remembered almost none except for Kate. And he remembered blond, smart, cynical Kate because she was nothing like his mother and nothing like the other proper women who were his mother's friends. Kate was a rebel.

Dante had a soft spot for rebels.

Daisy Collingsworth was another rebel. "Maybe we shouldn't talk. I think a dance would be better."

"I'd rather wait and dance with Carter."

Daisy had meant to prick his pride, and yet her words had the opposite effect. Dante laughed, a genuine laugh that exposed the smooth column of his bronze throat, and the rich sound rolled out, deep, sexy, very powerful. If all eyes weren't watching before, they were now.

His burning gaze slid over her, settling on her mouth. "Liar. You want to dance with me as much as I want to dance with you."

His suggestive tone sent shivers up and down her

spine, and her breasts ached, nipples hardening against the cool mesh of her top.

Shyly she glanced up, her eyes skimming past his perfect mouth to the smoky golden warmth of his eyes. She saw her reflection there, and she saw something else, something altogether new. *He wanted her.*

He wanted *her.*

It was a heady realization, and she felt her heart slow, her lips part.

His head dipped, and he cupped her cheek. She felt shivery and alive, and instinctively she lifted her face to his, eyes on his lips.

"Daisy," a voice interrupted, "your drink."

Carter had returned. Daisy took the cocktail glass from him. Dante stepped back—but not very far.

"No champagne?" Dante said.

Carter looked momentarily confused. "Daisy, did you want champagne?"

Daisy shot Dante a dark glance. What was he doing? Why did he want to cause trouble? "This is wonderful. I'm happy with a cocktail."

"I can get you champagne," Carter said more forcefully. "I didn't know you wanted champagne."

"I don't want champagne. I like my cocktail. Really." She could happily dump her drink over Dante. He was standing there enjoying Carter's discomfiture. Well, to hell with him. "Carter, would you like to dance?"

She caught the lift of Dante's eyebrows and was grateful when Carter moved forward, blocking Dante from her view. "Yes, let's. It's a nice slow song."

A slow song. Not what she wanted, but if it gave her some distance from Dante, then it was a good thing.

"Goodbye, Count," Carter said with a nod of his head.

"I'll catch up with you soon," Dante answered, still smiling, still looking infuriatingly amused.

Carter held her hand and led her through the enormous white party tent. A band played on a wooden stage, and white twinkling lights were strung from the tent poles.

They still held their drink glasses, and at the edge of the dance floor Carter faced her. "Let's toast the start of something wonderful."

Her hand shook slightly. "And what is that, Carter?"

"A great future."

Daisy felt like she was losing control. This wasn't working out the way she'd imagined. She shouldn't have come here tonight with Carter. This wasn't business. He was making the contract personal.

She set her glass down without drinking. "What about Kentucky Kiss?"

"Let's not ruin a lovely evening—"

"That's why I'm here, Carter. This is about Kentucky Kiss. This is about contracts and negotiations." She broke off as Peter Lindley bore down on them.

"Carter, hello," Mr. Lindley greeted. "Enjoying yourself?"

"It's a beautiful party. You couldn't ask for nicer weather. Peter, you know Daisy Collingsworth, I believe?"

Peter's smile faded perceptibly. His guard was instantly up, and he shifted away. "We've met."

Oh, yes, they'd met, Daisy thought, only about a thousand times. He'd been her father's best friend for nearly twenty years. "Good evening, Mr. Lindley."

"How are things?" he asked stiffly.

"Dad's doing fine."

Peter's jaw tensed, lips compressing. "I meant with regards to the farm."

"The stable's rebuilt," Carter interjected. "A state-of-the-art facility. Thirty-six stalls, and they're developing their stallion barn next."

Peter's forehead creased. "Is that true?"

Daisy opened her mouth, but Carter answered first again. "I'm considering moving my stallion to their barn." He shot Daisy a swift glance. "If things continue to improve as they have."

"What about trainers?" Peter rubbed his chin as he glanced from Daisy to Carter and back again. "Since McCaw passed on, you haven't had any big name on board. You need one. While there is considerable interest in your foal, no one will pay top dollar for a yearling that hasn't been started right."

McCaw meaning Teddy, who'd died in the fire. A lump filled her throat. "I'm aware of that." She was grateful she could keep her tone calm even if it was just an illusion, because right now on the inside she was miserable.

Peter nodded brusquely. "Fine. Best of luck." He turned to Carter. "May I have a word with you?"

Carter excused himself, and Daisy stood alone on the edge of the dance floor wondering yet again what she was doing at the Lindleys'.

"Your friend Carter could be a little more attentive."

Daisy turned and smiled. "Dante Galván, what a surprise."

"If you were my date, I'd never leave you alone."

Her smile stretched. "I'm not your date, and you haven't left me alone."

"Touché." A light shone in his eyes. His grin looked careless, devilish, relaxed. "Sequins and spurs, Daisy Collingsworth. You're a very intriguing woman."

"Kentucky Kiss can't mean all that much to you."

"Kentucky Kiss has nothing to do with this. I happen to like you."

His deep voice rumbled through her, rich and intoxicating, and she felt herself grow warm and weak. "The Collingsworths are trouble," she retorted, fighting for the right flippant note.

"I've always liked trouble." He lightly touched the small of her back. "Dance with me."

His hand burned through her sequin and mesh top. She felt herself grow impossibly warm. "Carter wouldn't like it."

"I'm not asking Carter to dance. I'm asking you." His palm slid down, coming to rest on her hip, his fingertips just brushing her bottom. "Would Daisy like it?"

She couldn't move, couldn't breathe, couldn't think. His hand felt incredible, and her body felt wildly sensitive. Suddenly she wanted to be daring and dangerous. She wanted to be all the things she'd never allowed herself to be.

A waiter carrying a tray of champagne flutes passed by. Dante reached out and lifted a glass from the tray and handed it to her. "If you're going to drink, you should drink champagne. The color suits you."

"The color?" Her voice was all but inaudible.

"Pale gold, crisp, not too sweet and yet full and ripe in the mouth." He lifted the glass, with her hand still on it, and drank.

She blushed at the intimacy of the gesture, and her skin glowed, taut and warm all over. "I think you're projecting, Count Galván."

"Call me count again and I'll kiss you here, in front of all these nice people."

Her blush deepened. "A promise, or a threat?"

His head dipped, and his lips brushed her cheek and then the curve of her ear. "You'd like it, Daisy."

She ought to be outraged. Instead she was captivated by the warmth of his breath against her ear and the feel of his lips against her cheek.

The crowd disappeared and the band faded to the background. Her head tipped and she gazed at him, momentarily lost in his intensely expressive eyes.

He was beautiful. Everything about him was hard and sensual. His face was a canvas of gorgeous lines and planes. Even his mouth had the perfect shape, the lower lip slightly thrust out with a small flat indentation.

She wanted him to kiss her, wanted to feel his mouth against hers.

Dante could see in her eyes that she wanted him to kiss her. He wanted to kiss her. He'd wanted to kiss her since he first confronted her at the track two days ago.

He flattened his palm against the curve of her bottom and urged her closer. Bending his head, he covered her lips with his and heard her inhale, an involuntary gasp at the burst of heat flaring between them. It wasn't his imagination. Daisy felt electric.

Her lips trembled beneath his, and he drew her closer, more fully against him even as he parted her lips to explore the inside of her mouth.

Daisy tasted warm and sweet, like clover honey, and gradually she curved into him until she fit him perfectly. He kissed her until he forgot where they were, forgot himself, kissed her until his body surged to life, threatening to betray him. And just realizing how close he was to losing control cut through the passion like a knife, forcing him to take an immediate step back.

Daisy blinked at Dante in confusion. The kiss had sent hot, sharp darts shooting from her lips to every nerve in her body. Her brain felt cloudy, and she struggled to clear the fog. What had just happened?

But before she could do anything, say anything, Carter Scott returned, and Daisy could tell by his tense expression that he'd seen the kiss.

Carter made a grab at Daisy. "I know you're something of a playboy, count, but I have to say, you're taking it a bit far with my date."

Daisy reddened. "Carter—"

"No, I'll handle this, Daisy," he interrupted coldly. "I suggest you leave, Galván, you've worn out your welcome."

"This isn't your party," Dante answered, thrusting his hands in his black trouser pockets. "And I have no desire to leave. Things are just getting interesting."

Carter stiffened. "Then we'll go."

"Maybe you want to wait until we've discussed business first. That's why you're here, isn't it? So you and Daisy can make plans for Kentucky Kiss's future?"

"Dante, please," Daisy protested huskily, wondering how a night could get much worse. "Let's not do this here."

"Why not? Carter likes to mix business and pleasure. Especially when it comes to the beautiful Collingsworth sisters."

Daisy felt faint. *"Dante."*

"You really have some nerve, Galván," Carter shot back, slamming his cocktail glass to the damask-covered table. "I've known Bill Collingsworth forever."

"But this isn't about Bill. It's about his daughters and the fact that you're hiding your true intentions behind a pseudo Southern gentleman persona."

"I resent that! Bill and I go back a long, long way, and I happen to care a great deal about his family."

Dante's smile was thin, hard. "I imagine you would."

"While it's none of your business, the arrangements I've made with the Collingsworth family are legal and beneficial. They will profit. Substantially."

"And what do you get out of it?" Dante returned, folding his arms across his chest.

"I get to breed my stallion with a champion mare. This is about horses and only horses."

"Then if it's that simple, you shouldn't have a problem working with me. Daisy is selling Kentucky Kiss to me, and I'd be more than willing to renegotiate the contract with you. In fact, I'll give you a better deal than the Collingsworths." Dante's eyes narrowed, his mouth slanted. "You're an honest businessman. How can you object to that?"

"But why should I go to the trouble of renegotiating a contract if I already have one in place?" Carter was flustered.

"Because as you said, you're a good friend of the family's and you and Bill Collingsworth go way, way back," he said, drawing out the words with stinging emphasis. "And good friends like to help each other out."

Carter's complexion looked pasty. "This is manipulation."

"This is business. I'm offering you a better deal."

Dante wasn't going to budge. He knew what he wanted, he wanted what he wanted, and he fought until he had it.

Daisy looked at him, the air still bottled in her lungs, her nerves screaming on edge, and knew he'd won.

He was a man who picked his battles carefully. He only fought for what he believed in and then he only fought the battles he knew he could win.

He knew he could beat Carter Scott. And he had.

CHAPTER FIVE

DANTE offered to drive Daisy home, and since Carter had abandoned her, she accepted the offer. Inside his car, she reached for her seat belt and then grimaced with pain.

"Still hurts?" he said, watching her struggle with her seat belt.

He leaned toward her, one long arm extended, and grasped the silver tab of the seat belt, pulling the strap secure. She felt his nose and mouth brush her hair, and her stomach tightened, a hot desire coiling in her belly.

"That'll teach you to fight," he said, lifting her hand and inspecting the swelling.

A knot formed in her throat. His touch made her feel almost frantic. "Please, not another lecture."

Dante saw the emotion darken her eyes, her skin heating with a desire she hadn't fully come to terms with. Well, that made two of them, he thought savagely, torn between duty and desire.

He wanted nothing more than to draw her onto his lap and kiss the creamy line of her jaw and the hollow beneath her ear. He wanted to touch his tongue to the rapid pulse at the base of her neck.

But he couldn't do it. Not now, not the way things were between them.

Frustration roughened his voice. "If you're going to throw punches, you should at least know how to fight. I'm surprised your father didn't teach you."

"He didn't approve of girls fighting."

"Smart man." Dante knew he should start the car but he couldn't stop looking at her. Her mouth was so soft. Her skin so sensitive. He just wanted to give her one kiss, there, on the corner of her lips.

But that one kiss wouldn't be enough. He'd be driven to kiss her lower lip and then the incredibly soft side of her neck and— He turned the engine on. Scruples! He bit back an oath and shifted into gear. The car roared down the driveway.

Daisy's soft voice penetrated his dark mood. "I thought you hated my dad."

"I hate irresponsibility," he said after a moment, easing his foot off the accelerator. "But I don't hate your dad. However, I don't think he did you any favors by retiring when the farm was deep in debt."

He was about to continue when he caught a glimpse of her face reflected in the glass. She'd turned to look out the window, and he saw worry in her eyes, saw pain there, too. Daisy Collingsworth wasn't all that tough.

Dante flexed one hand against the steering wheel, muscles tight with tension. Being alone with her was going to drive him mad.

"If you must throw a punch," he said tersely, eyes on the road, the car's headlights cutting through the darkness, illuminating scattered oak trees and miles of fence, "the power has to come from here." He tapped her shoulder. "Never your wrist."

Just the touch of his fingers on her bare shoulder made her ache. He was winding her up, turning her into a quivering ball of need. She was in over her head. But it had nothing to do with horses and debts. It was Dante. He was doing this to her. No other man had turned her inside out like this. She knew how to handle a spirited horse but she knew nothing about managing a virile, sexual man. Which was why working with Dante could be a disaster. If she wasn't careful, he could—would—take advantage of her.

In front of her house he killed the engine and Daisy saw the front door of the farm house open and close. What was Zoe doing up?

She swung open her door, moonlight reflecting off her sequin top, casting shimmering dots against the car.

"Rosie, is that you?"

Daisy's heart faltered. Dad. What was he doing outside at this time of night?

Conscious of Dante slowly climbing from the car, she rushed toward the house, high heels clicking against the brick walk. "Daddy, go inside."

But her father moved forward into the light. "Who's there?"

"Dad, it's me, Daisy. Go inside." She couldn't let Dante see her father like this. Her father's pajamas weren't lined up straight, the blue and burgundy pin-stripes going off in different directions. His hair was messy and his eyes vacant. She tried to push him into the house but he wouldn't move. "Daddy, please."

"Bill, do you have a minute?" Dante said sharply. He'd recognized her father and sounded angry.

"No, he doesn't," she retorted, shooting Dante a furious glance over her bare shoulder. She wouldn't let her dad get drawn into this, wouldn't let him face anyone's ridicule. She held his hand between hers. "Go inside now. Please."

"But I thought I heard a car," her father said.

"You did. It was Dante Galván's," she choked, feeling a sense of doom. Things just kept getting worse.

"Who?"

"Dante Galván, from Buenos Aires."

"Don't know him."

She saw Dante from the corner of her eye. His eyes were narrowed, his expression impossible to read. "It's okay, Dad, and it's late. Let me take you in."

"Where's your mother?"

Chest tight, heart aching, Daisy reached up to smooth the puckered pajama top. "Mom's gone, Dad."

"But she's coming home soon."

Her mother had been gone for twenty years. She'd died when Daisy was four, just hours after Zoe was born.

"Not that soon," she answered gently, hating to see the confusion in his eyes, his eyes the same light blue shade as hers. Zoe's irises were more lavender, while Daisy's and her father's were glacier blue. "Let's go upstairs. Get you back to bed. Okay?"

Dante was waiting for her in the front hall when she came downstairs.

He didn't speak, and she didn't look at him. She stood there, waiting for whatever would come next.

A minute passed and then another. She couldn't stand

it, had to get through whatever pity—or scorn—he might express. She looked up. Dante's expression was sober.

"He's sick," Dante said quietly.

"Yes. Alzheimer's."

"He's been ill for awhile."

Daisy didn't answer, and Dante continued. "He must have been ill when he signed the contract with my father."

"I imagine so." She was so tired she was shaking.

"You should have told me." He sounded angry, but whether with her or Tino, she didn't know. "My father destroyed dozens of people with his greed. Chaos and destruction. That was my father's legacy."

Daisy clasped her arms around her. She felt moved to tears but she didn't cry. She hadn't cried in nearly twenty years. "I'm sorry."

"No, I'm sorry. My father took advantage of your father. It makes me sick. It makes me—" he broke off, shook his head. "I swear to you, Daisy, I will not let my father's legacy continue. His greed stops here. I cannot let his avarice destroy you."

Overnight Dante took control of their lives.

He hired a housekeeper and a part-time nurse and sent for Clemente, one of his managers from his Argentina *estancia*.

"We can't afford the help," Daisy protested on learning what he'd done. She felt increasingly vulnerable. It was one thing to get help for Zoe and the house, but to send for his manager? He wasn't going to replace her, was he?

"I'm paying the salaries," he answered, dismissing her worries. "I can afford it."

"But we'll never pay you back."

"No, you won't, but the farm will. We'll restructure the contract between Galván Enterprises and Collingsworth Farm."

So it had happened. The farm was no longer a private family business. Dante was in charge. Daisy swallowed the lump in her throat. "So what will I be doing?" she whispered.

"Taking a crash course in farm management."

"Where?"

"Argentina."

Daisy did a double-take. "You've got to be kidding."

"I couldn't be more serious."

He was serious. Nearly forty-eight hours later she was boarding his jet at dawn at Lexington's executive airport. But she was still fighting him every inch of the way. "I don't see the point in dragging me to Argentina to work your ranch when I have a farm of my own," she said, settling into her leather seat.

"Management isn't an innate skill, it's an acquired knowledge, something that must be learned."

"Yes, but I could learn at home. Under Clemente."

"Felipe Gutierrez, my *estancia* manager, trained Clemente. He'll train you. He is the best." Dante took out a newspaper and turned his attention to the text.

Obviously, in his mind, the discussion was over.

Daisy wanted to argue but knew she'd already lost the battle. She was on the plane, wasn't she?

They flew from Kentucky to Miami where they were

scheduled to refuel before making the long hop to
Buenos Aires.

Unfortunately, flying into Miami proved disastrous.
Within an hour after arriving, hurricane warnings forced
Miami's air traffic control to temporarily shut down the
runways.

Dante was immediately on his cell phone, pacing the
executive terminal and making a stream of calls. He
spoke in Spanish, a language Daisy had studied in high
school for two years, which meant she could order a
meal but not much else. Yet she didn't need to speak
his language to know he was furious, and with each
successive phone call his voice grew sharper and his
expression darker. Something was definitely wrong.

As he paced, Daisy overheard him say a woman's
name not just once or twice, but repeatedly. Then he
snapped his phone closed. The phone rang again, he answered even more curtly, and again he ended the call
abruptly.

She didn't know what the issue was, but somehow
she knew he'd win in the end. He picked his battles
carefully, focused on the outcome and persevered.

Like with Carter at the Lindleys'. And then with her
and the farm contract. When she'd met him yesterday at
Pembroke, Pembroke and Brown, he knew exactly what
he wanted and he got it. He was nothing if not shrewd.

With the new contract, he'd positioned himself as the
controlling investor in Collingsworth Farm, owning a
majority interest. He'd receive eighty percent of the future returns and would have the final say in all issues
relating to farm operations, including replacing Daisy as

farm manager in six months' time if he didn't feel proper progress was being made.

He hadn't resorted to blackmail, she thought ruefully, watching him pocket his cell phone, but he'd come awfully close.

Dante turned and faced her. But he wasn't looking at her. At least, he wasn't seeing her. He was miles away, lost in thought. She'd never seen him so troubled and she resisted feeling a twinge of sympathy. If he hadn't played hardball with her over the farm contract, she might have more empathy, but he was tough. He deserved what he got.

Suddenly he looked at her and saw her watching him. The heavy crease between his brows eased, and his jaw relaxed into a reluctant smile.

Her heart did a funny little flip. Why it did, she didn't know, but even her pulse quickened and her lips curved into a reluctant smile.

He walked toward her, stopped in front of her chair. "I haven't been good company," he said rather apologetically.

She saw the fatigue in his expression, creases fanning from his eyes. He really did look tired. "Problems at home?" she guessed.

"Always." He laughed and shook his head. "My family is like a soap opera. Nothing but crisis and melodrama."

He made her smile. "Sounds interesting."

"If unstable." His grin stretched, a self-deprecating grin that made him look incredibly charming and incredibly dangerous. "But I've never minded challenges."

Somehow she sensed he wasn't just referring to his family.

Once the hurricane warnings were lifted they were allowed to take off. Six hours after takeoff the Gulfstream jet made its final descent, dropping through a brilliant glaze of late afternoon sun and startling blue sky. Daisy leaned toward the window, gazing out the plane window at the clear horizon and the endless green and gold land. The ground loomed closer, and the plane's wings dipped then righted.

The jet touched down on the runway in a series of little hops, gradually reducing speed until it rolled to a complete stop.

"Someone from the *estancia* will be picking us up," Dante said, opening the Gulfstream's door and jumping out. "The pilot radioed ahead. Shouldn't be long now."

Daisy recoiled at the blanket of heat as she stepped off the plane. Unlike the warm humid American South, the climate was hot and dry and the high temperature seemed to swallow her whole.

It looked as though they'd landed in the middle of nowhere. The airstrip cut straight through what appeared to be one endless pasture. She saw nothing for miles but grass. Just a distant line of scrubby trees marked the horizon. She shaded her eyes, squinting against the sun. "Where are we again?"

"About five miles from the house."

"The land is endless."

"This is the pampas." He rolled up his shirtsleeves,

revealing sinewy tendons and tanned forearms, and quickly unloaded the luggage from the tail of the plane.

The pilot and plane had been gone for over an hour, and despite Dante's assurances, no one had arrived for them. Daisy took a seat on her battered suitcase, propped her boots on another and made herself comfortable.

"I'm sorry about this." Dante's tone was clipped, his embarrassment tangible. "Someone should have been here by now, which leads me to believe that there's been a bit of a problem."

Daisy's wide, curious gaze induced him to explain. "Anabella," he said. "My sister. I have three sisters, but Anabella is the pill. My constant headache. She is more trouble than all the Galváns put together."

Yet despite his cynical words, Daisy heard the tenderness in his voice. He loved his sister. Very much. "Perhaps it's not really Anabella creating the problem."

"It's because I know her and love her I can safely say this delay is Anabella's fault. This has never happened before. Not in ten years of flying in and out of the ranch."

"Can you call someone?"

"I don't get cellular coverage here. No towers in the area yet. I intend to bring them in, though. In fact, that's what I'm working on now."

Daisy tossed a small pebble. "We can always walk."

"Not an option. Can't leave the luggage and too much to carry."

"But what if no one comes?"

"Someone will come. I'm expected."

Daisy struggled not to smile. "Yes, obviously."

He shot her a quick look, black eyebrows rising. "What was that you said, *muneca?*"

He was looking at her, really looking at her, and she felt his size, his strength and his focus. His attention was as thrilling as it was unnerving. She still had no idea how to handle his blatant virility.

Suddenly whatever they were talking about was less interesting, less important than what was happening between them. Daisy shifted on the suitcase, put her feet down, bracing her. "I, uh…"

He took a small step toward her. "Yes?"

She wanted him to touch her. She wanted him to close the distance between them, wrap his hands around her arms and drag her close. She wanted to feel him pressed hard against her, and her throat swelled closed, her body throbbing, heart hammering.

She thought he must feel her, because she certainly felt him. She felt an energy, an awareness that she'd never felt from anyone before.

Daisy swallowed hard, pressed her hands to her thighs, struggled to calm her turbulent emotions. She'd never survive a night here at this rate, much less six weeks.

"Daisy?"

No one had ever said her name that way before. He made her feel sexy, desirable. "Yes?"

His gaze was intense. He seemed to be staring into her, searching for something, and yet she didn't know what he wanted to find. "This can't happen here, Daisy."

Her mouth turned dry. She blinked to focus on him better.

"Anabella is very…impressionable."

"Most teenage girls are," she answered faintly.

"Yes, but not all are quite so self-destructive. Anabella is on a crash course with disaster." He hesitated, tension rolling off him in waves. "I'm responsible for her."

Daisy felt warmth creep beneath her skin. "I understand."

"Do you?"

His inflection made her quiver. Did she understand? He had to be a good brother, a role model, responsible. He was going to do the right thing.

But what did that have to do with her?

Dante was waiting for her to answer. She mustered a smile, feeling both awkward and unsure of herself. She wasn't sure what he wanted from her. "Actually, maybe I don't understand. How does your responsibility for Anabella impact me?"

"This—us," he said bluntly, gesturing toward her, "won't work here."

She couldn't have been more shocked or embarrassed. He wasn't serious, was he? And if he was, he had no right suggesting or projecting. They'd exchanged a kiss at the Lindleys'. Big deal. It signified nothing. She'd been kissed before and hadn't planned a wedding.

"I think you're worried about nothing," she said tightly. She'd been clenching her teeth trying to stay calm and her jaw had begun to ache with the effort. "I'm not looking for romance, and if I did, I wouldn't look to you."

Color flared in his cheekbones. "I could make you eat your words."

"That wasn't a dare, Dante, just a statement of fact. You like to think that you've got me—and life—all figured out. Well, you don't. You might be able to control yourself, but you can't control others, and you certainly can't control me. I'm here for one reason and one reason only—to work with Señor Gutierrez and learn how to run a more efficient stable."

His amber eyes blazed, and she ignored the whisper in her head that said she was being too confrontational, too Daisy.

"You are attracted to me," he insisted.

"Just like I'm attracted to a thousand other men. But I don't chase them and I don't hop into bed with them. So you can relax, count, you're safe with me."

Suddenly he was moving toward her and lifting her to her feet. Just his hands on her arms made her shiver, but when his leg bumped her knee, wedging her feet apart, she gasped for air.

"What was that?" he murmured, his mouth near her ear, his lips brushing her skin as he drew her close against him, hip to hip. "Were you eating your words, maybe?"

She shuddered at the feel of his chest against her breasts. He was warm and hard where she was soft. It was delicious and torturous at the same time. "Not a chance."

"False courage is worse than no courage," he taunted,

shifting slightly, and just that subtle swing of his hips made her sinfully aware of his arousal. She ached in every place he touched, and fireworks exploded beneath her skin.

Helplessly she sucked in a breath, her head spinning, senses reeling, every nerve in her so taut and alive that she felt as though she'd burst out of her skin any moment. "You're the one making assumptions."

"I'm not making assumptions. I want you. You know I want you, but we can't have an affair because it's not the right example to set for Anabella."

Fire-hot shivers raced through her. She'd never felt so heated before. "No. We can't have one because I don't want one with you!"

"You can't admit the truth."

"The truth is we're only together now because we're stuck with the lousy decisions our fathers made. We have nothing in common, we would have never been attracted to each other if we weren't forced to work together, and this…this energy or chemistry or whatever you want to call it isn't real."

He laughed grimly. "It's as real as anything else in life, *muneca*."

"Well, I don't feel a thing." And that was a lie, she thought, because her legs had melted and her body felt like honey and she wanted him so badly she thought she'd pop out of her skin.

He knew she was lying, too.

His eyes darkened, his head shook once and then his mouth covered hers in a hard punishing kiss, a kiss that stole her breath, clouded her head and turned her legs to mush.

His tongue thrust against the edge of her teeth, flicked the inside of her lower lip, and when she opened her mouth to him plundered the warm, moist recesses.

The incredibly sexual thrusting of his tongue gave her a graphic idea of what his body would do to hers given the chance, and she shuddered in response, desire surging through her in wild, unmitigated waves.

A moan of frustration escaped her, and he arched her backward, dragging her hips tight against his hard groin and pressing her chest. It was a strangely vulnerable position and yet also exciting.

He made her feel so hot and sensitive that when his hand slid beneath her blue cotton blouse she nearly fainted at the exquisite pleasure of his palm against her bare skin.

His touch was electric, erotic. His fingertips seemed to count and measure her ribs before cupping her breasts. This desire was something altogether new, something so wild and desperate that Daisy couldn't think, just feel. She felt his palm graze her nipple over the lace cup of her bra and then peel the lace away and rub the nipple.

Her body had taken over; her need had a will of its own. She loved the newness of her desire, loved the intensity, as well. She'd never thought she could feel so much, hadn't expected her hunger to be so strong.

With one hand he cupped her bottom and urged her closer to his hips, pressing her against his straining body.

Sweet mercy. Her gasp left him in no doubt as to her feelings, nor did her helpless response as his hips ground against hers, his arousal pressing between her thighs, striking the most tender of nerves.

Her breasts felt heavy, the nipples thrusting against her shirt, her thighs clenched, desire throbbing in her belly. She'd strip here, if he wanted. She'd strip him, too, and—

A car horn blared in the distance, over and over, as though the driver were leaning on it.

Daisy heard the noise in a dim part of her brain and managed to ignore it. But Dante heard it and with a guttural groan pulled away.

"This is real," he said thickly, as she swayed on her feet and clung to his arms, "but this is what can't happen. Not here. Not in Argentina, and especially near my sister. *Comprehende?*"

He was furious, but whether with her or himself she couldn't tell. She stared into his eyes, saw the fire mix with anger, desire with frustration and knew he was right. This was not a good thing and couldn't be encouraged, much less permitted.

"*Comprehende,*" she replied, pushing back from him, her face warm, her body throbbing.

He'd obliterated her self-control completely. Turned her inside out and reduced her to a puddle of need. Incredible.

The car horn sounded again, and Dante lifted a hand in greeting as a dark green Land Rover jostled and gyrated into view.

"My sister," he said grimly, turning to face Daisy and attempting to tuck the hem of her blouse into her trousers.

She brushed his hand away. "Don't worry. This won't happen again."

His lips compressed. He glanced at the clouds of dust encircling the car and then at Daisy. "You understand why?"

She shoved the shirttail inside her waistband and adjusted her silver belt buckle. "Yes. Because I don't want this to happen again."

"That's not the issue."

"It is the issue. Your father and my father screwed up, and we've been left to sort it out. So let's sort it out so I can go home and get the hell out of Argentina!" She heard her voice crack, felt her composure shatter. She was on the edge, more than on the edge and very close to losing all self-control.

His kiss, his hands, his touch…they undid her. Worse than undid her.

He made her want so much—*too much*—and she didn't know how to cope with such intense sensations and emotions. It was one thing to be attracted to someone but it was another to feel utterly carnal. And she felt carnal. She felt hungry and raw and desperate.

Heaven help her, this was not how it was supposed to be, at all.

CHAPTER SIX

THE green car careened to a stop, kicking up dirt and loose pebbles. The driver leaned out the window, arms braced against the door, long black hair tumbling past bare shoulders. "*Hola*, Dante," the teenage girl shouted.

"You're late," Dante snapped.

"Not very. A half hour. Maybe an hour."

She'd been speaking Spanish, but Dante abruptly switched to English. "Two hours late, Anabella. You were supposed to be here at four."

Anabella switched easily to English, too, her accent surprisingly mild. She'd obviously spent considerable time in the States.

"You said five," Anabella insisted. "I come up at five." Her slim shoulders lifted, fell in a graceful little shrug. "Four. Five. Sounds the same, no? Maybe I misunderstood."

"They don't sound the same to most people," Dante answered, teeth flashing, jaw jutting, making Daisy think of a lion snarling.

"But I'm not most people."

Daisy was sure he was going to lose his temper. He looked perfectly furious. And then suddenly the tension melted from his body, the anger fading from his features.

"No, you're not like most people. That's the problem with you."

She shot him a naughty, teasing glance, green-gold eyes dancing with mischief. "It's good to see you, too, Dante."

"You are supposed to be in school. What happened?"

"They threw me out. Again. Can you believe that?" She made a face at him, chin propped on the window-frame. Her eyes were a lighter shade than Dante's and considerably greener, but she was every bit as beautiful and perhaps even more vivid.

No wonder Dante had his hands full. Anabella wasn't just physically perfect, she was mentally quick, her tone, gestures, features alive and vivacious.

"Unfortunately, I can believe it," he answered, leaning forward and kissing her on each cheek. "Now get in the back, I'm going to drive home."

"Let me drive!"

"Anabella."

In the end, she reluctantly climbed over the seat, her tight black skirt hiked high on her thigh revealing an extraordinary amount of leg. Although Dante cast her outfit a disapproving glance, he didn't directly comment on it.

Anabella had him wrapped around her gorgeous little finger.

In the car, luggage loaded and Dante behind the wheel driving them home, Anabella leaned forward to get a better look at Daisy.

"So *you're* the new girlfriend," Anabella announced,

curiosity in her voice. "An American girlfriend. Just like Daddy used to have."

Daisy shot Dante an uneasy glance. Their father had girlfriends?

Dante's eyebrows lowered. "Ana, not in front of strangers."

"But she's not a stranger if she's your girlfriend!"

"Daisy is not my girlfriend," he answered tersely. "She's here to work with Señor Gutierrez. It's business."

"Ah, business." But Anabella's arch expression indicated disbelief. "This is what you always say, Dante. Everything is business, but I know you are not a priest. You are too beautiful to be a priest."

"Anabella!"

Dante sounded strangled. Daisy almost felt pity for him. Almost, but not quite.

Anabella smiled. Leaning against Daisy's seat, she whispered to her, "Dante loves women. But he doesn't get serious. Lots of women but no serious girlfriends and no wedding. He is too busy with business."

"Ana!" Dante's voice thundered through the car. Switching to Spanish, he gave his baby sister an earful, but Anabella shrugged and looked out the window.

After several tense, silent minutes Anabella sighed. "I hate the *estancia*. I don't know why you keep this place, Dante. It makes me crazy here. Everything's so slow."

"It might be good for you to take things slow for awhile," he said cryptically.

His sister tossed her head. "I can take things slow when I die, and I'm not dead yet."

"You will be, if you continue to live so recklessly."

Anabella didn't say anything for a long moment, and then with a jerk she pulled herself forward, taking a seat on the center console. Her long hair hung in her eyes and she pushed it away with an impatient flick of her wrist. "You're not going to leave me here, Dante. It's just for the weekend, right? That's what the driver said when he picked me up. Just for the weekend." Her voice began to rise in panic and frustration. "You know I hate it here. Promise me I'm going back to the city with you on Sunday."

Dante kept his eyes fixed on the pale dirt road ahead. "I can't make that promise, Ana."

Anabella let out a piercing cry. "You can't keep me here. I'm not a prisoner. You can't make me a prisoner."

"I'm not making you a prisoner."

"You are if you keep me here. You know how I go crazy here."

"We're not going to talk about it now."

"Well, *I* am." She slammed her hand down, rattling the console. "This isn't my home. I want to go to Mama's."

"You know it's not an option."

"I'm almost eighteen. I can do what I want."

"Not a chance."

"Dante!"

"Enough! I don't want to hear another word. Discussion over."

Anabella fell back onto the seat and covered her face with her hands. No one spoke for the remainder of the journey.

Dante drove faster, gunning the motor as though chased by the devil, and maybe in a way he was, Daisy thought, clinging to the Land Rover seat, her silvery hair swirling in her eyes. Obviously they shared many family secrets, secrets that continued to haunt both Dante and Anabella.

The car bounced and jolted its way toward the distant line of trees. Closer, the trees loomed larger and rounder, the lush, leafy trees becoming a magnificent alley of shade that ended before a vast Spanish colonial mansion.

Drawing up in front of the house, Dante parked and turned off the engine. "My home," he said, gesturing toward the elaborate whitewashed facade.

The bell tower's red tiled roof gleamed almost copper beneath the early evening sun and reminded her of one of the missions in the American Southwest.

Daisy opened her door. "It's not a new house built to look old?"

"No, it's just naturally old," Anabella sullenly interjected, jumping out and stomping up the front steps. "You won't find anything new here. No television, no movies, no video or computer games. Just one hundred and eighty years of old."

The front door shook as Anabella slammed it shut.

"And that," Dante said flatly, grabbing the suitcases from the back, "is sweet Anabella."

Dante was a beast.

A gorgeous beast, Daisy conceded, toweling off and dressing, putting on a pair of linen trousers the color of wheat and a matching sleeveless knit top.

He was a gorgeous beast who knew far more than she did about making love and happened to use his expertise on her with nerve-shattering ease. Just thinking about the kiss on the airstrip made her stomach do a fabulous flip-flop. He was skilled and doubly deadly because in this area he had far more control than she did, and if Daisy hated anything, it was weakness.

He made her weak. He made her crave things she couldn't have, especially not from him.

The one and only time she'd been intimate with a man hadn't been a disaster, but it hadn't turned her into a vixen, either. He was a nice guy in her university program and they'd gone together for awhile before finally making love. She was twenty-one and ready to lose her virginity, but in the end, he hadn't been the best choice. It wasn't particularly awful. It just wasn't particularly good. She'd gone through the motions, and that's what it had been. Motions without any emotions. Some pelvic gyrations on his part, which left her rather…cold.

She'd decided she wasn't the passionate sort. After all, she'd waited this long to have sex, she must not have a strong drive.

But Dante was making her reconsider that drive. In fact, he was forcing her to reconsider quite a few of her closely held beliefs.

Daisy put down her brush and stared at her reflection. Just because she felt attracted to him didn't mean she could have, or should have, a relationship with him. Besides, did he really think he was the only one that cared about responsibility? She had just as strong a sense of duty and obligation as he did. Probably stronger.

So there. Nothing was going to happen because she didn't want anything to happen. And that's the way it was.

Now all she had to do was face him.

Outside her bedroom, Daisy was directed by one of the housemaids to the covered, lit patio where she discovered Dante waiting for her. The dining room's French doors had been opened to welcome the cooler evening air, and pots of blooming citrus trees marked the long veranda at regular intervals.

He'd also showered and changed and was dressed in light chino slacks and a caramel knit shirt open at the collar. The caramel color was gorgeous on him, played up his thick dark hair, warm toffee eyes and the touch of bronze in his skin.

Beast, she muttered silently, feeling her heart begin to thump harder. ''Where's Anabella?'' Daisy asked, not wanting to be alone with him, not the way she was feeling at the moment.

''She'll be here soon.''

''I'll go check on her.''

''No need. I asked her to give us fifteen minutes alone.''

Daisy stiffened and slowly turned to face him. ''Why?''

His gaze held hers. ''Don't play dumb. It's obvious we need to sort a few things out before I leave tomorrow.''

He was leaving already? Disappointment surged through her. Aware of his scrutiny she half-turned away, trying to cover her chaotic emotions. "What do we need to sort out?"

"For a woman who prefers honesty, you've certainly developed a taste for ambiguity."

She blushed, swallowed, then acknowledged the truth in that. "What happened on the airstrip was a mistake."

"It might have been impulsive, but it wasn't a mistake."

The caress in his voice was unmistakable. He stole her breath. Trapped her heart in his hands. She coughed, backed up a step. "But you said—"

"I never said I wasn't attracted to you. I said we couldn't have an affair, not while you're here."

"I don't want an affair."

"You do want me."

She shook her head, horrifyingly aware of her needs and desires. She'd never discussed something so private before. "It was just the heat of the moment."

His eyes narrowed and swept her hips, her breasts, her face. "Daisy, *we* are the heat of the moment."

She felt herself grow hot, even more sensitive, acutely sensitive in her arms, legs, fingers. Her belly felt tight and heavy. Her blood raced. "I think I forgot something in my room."

"Don't be a coward." His husky voice followed her as she started to flee.

Daisy froze, pressed her hands to her tummy, wondered how things had gotten so out of control. "Don't call me that. I'm not a coward. I've never been a coward."

"Then don't run away from me. We need to get this

sorted out before it becomes a problem. There's too much at stake. For both of us.''

Her heart thumped harder. She didn't understand her fear or her anxiety. ''It won't become a problem. I promise.''

''You can't make a promise like that.''

''Why not?''

''Come here. I'll show you.''

She turned, looked at him over her shoulder, her eyes wide. The corner of his mouth lifted, cynical and knowing. ''I won't touch you,'' he taunted softly. ''Just come, stand here. I'll show you what I mean.''

He gestured her forward, prompting her closer inch by inch until she stood an arm's length away.

The fine hair on her arms rose, skin prickling with awareness. She felt him, felt his heat and energy, and they were still two feet apart.

Her heart, which had been pounding a moment ago, seemed to stop, change rhythm and start beating again, this time more slowly.

''Feel that?'' he asked, his voice deeper than before, huskier, with a sensual appreciation she couldn't possibly ignore.

She couldn't admit it, and wouldn't admit it to him, but yes, she did feel him. It was the most intense current, a connection she couldn't explain.

Energy, desire, hunger.

In his arms she'd go places she'd never been. But in his arms she'd also lose control, and if she lost control terrible things might happen. Destruction. Chaos. The loss of the family farm.

Daisy couldn't risk it, no matter what she personally longed for.

The sun had gone, and the blue sky had long deepened with shades of lavender and gold. Daisy's fingers itched to touch his clean-shaven jaw, feel the muscles rippling beneath his shirt. But she didn't. "No. I don't feel anything."

His expression didn't change. Not even a flicker in his eyes, but his gaze held her captive, pinned her in place. He might as well have called her a liar because it was there in his eyes, there in the twist of his lips.

"Feel what?" Anabella asked, making a sudden appearance.

Daisy took a jerky step and turned. Anabella was dressed in a slim red silk sheath that merged into a bright orange band at her feet. It was a stunning dress on her, a simple cut but of such vibrant color that the girl fairly exuded heat.

"The heat," Daisy choked.

Anabella was oblivious to the undercurrents. "If you think this is hot, wait until January," the girl answered, pouring herself a glass of juice. "January sizzles."

Sizzles, Daisy repeated silently, catching the lift of Dante's eyebrows. She could just imagine life on the *estancia* then.

They were called to dinner. Anabella and Dante appeared to have patched things up. They chatted during the meal and several times Anabella slipped into Spanish, but Dante would reply in English for Daisy's sake.

Anabella shared a story about something that happened at school, drawing soft laughter from Dante.

Daisy furtively watched Dante as he listened to Anabella's story.

He really was lovely. She liked looking at him, listening to his voice, watching him interact with his sister. He was a benevolent big brother, part doting, part disciplinarian, but his love was tangible.

Dante looked up, caught her staring, and his lips twisted. He touched a finger to his mouth, and she stared at his lips in fascination. She loved the way his mouth felt against hers. She loved the way he kissed her. It was the most right feeling in the world.

His mouth curved into a crooked smile, and she wondered if he knew what she was thinking. He couldn't possibly sense her craving, could he?

His lashes suddenly lowered but not before she saw the speculative gleam in his eyes. He knew, she thought, drawing a breath, he knew. And he'd have something to say about it later.

Dinner over, Anabella asked to be excused to call a girlfriend in the city. Dante let her leave, and yet when Daisy asked to be excused, he refused.

"We haven't had coffee yet," he answered. "It's a nice evening, too. Let's sit outside, where it's cool."

Daisy didn't want to follow him, didn't want to go anywhere near him, but didn't have a choice.

He took a seat on a wood bench outside, a two-seater with no other chairs nearby.

The maid appeared with a tray. She placed the tray

on the bench next to Dante. Silently she poured the coffee before bowing her head and leaving.

Dante held a cup to Daisy. "Yours."

She started to refuse the cup, not because coffee didn't sound good but because she didn't feel comfortable risking contact. Yet the moment she realized her fear, she was determined to conquer it.

Daisy took the cup quickly, avoiding touching any part of him, and retreated to another bench.

He took a sip of his coffee and watched her sit down before leaning forward, powerful thighs straining his trousers. "Daisy, you're not as tough as you like to think."

His voice in the darkness sounded like honey, sweet rich, impossibly smooth. He'd snare her and she'd be trapped, stuck, caught in silken threads. Like the spider and the fly.

She hated the wildness of her heart. "What time do you leave tomorrow?"

She felt his smile. "Sometime in the morning, after I get you squared away with Señor Gutierrez. I'll be taking Anabella with me."

"She doesn't like it here much, does she?"

"She likes social activity. There's not much of that here." He hesitated, and the silence stretched between them. Finally, "You'll be all right here on your own?"

Was that what he was worried about? "I'll be fine. Unlike your sister, I'm not a city person. I prefer working and I like being out of doors."

"Your sister mentioned just before we left that you'd been to medical school."

"Veterinary medicine, yes."

"But you had to drop out?"

She shrugged, pretending an indifference she didn't feel. "I was needed at home."

"Maybe you'll be able to resume your studies after things settle down."

Things settle down? Did he mean after her father died?

She suddenly felt very tired, the long trip catching up with her. "It's late. I should go to bed, especially if I'm going to get up early to meet Señor Gutierrez."

He must have heard the fatigue in her voice and the way it cracked a little. Dante also rose. "Second thought, sleep in tomorrow. There's really no reason I can't postpone my trip by a few hours and introduce you to him over lunch. You need the rest."

"I don't need the rest. I need to learn. Remember? So, I'll set my alarm and be ready by six."

"No one is awake here at six, Daisy. This is Argentina."

"I'm willing to bet that Señor Gutierrez is awake at six."

"Yes, but—"

"Fine. I'll be up, too." She set her cup and saucer on the cart. "Good night, Dante."

"Good night, Daisy."

She was up early. Daisy dressed in her still-dark room and, aided with directions from a sleepy housemaid, found the stables just as the sun broke on the horizon.

Inside the stables a half dozen ranch hands were already busy at work.

Daisy immediately liked Señor Gutierrez. He was an older man, wiry, strong and grizzled from a lifetime in the sun. The morning passed quickly, and at noon Daisy returned to the house for lunch. But on reaching the house she discovered it empty. Dante and Anabella had already gone.

There weren't really words, she thought, for the emptiness she felt on learning that Dante had left on time after all, and without saying goodbye. She felt utterly flattened. Not to mention rejected.

It wasn't that she expected a big emotional farewell, but some kind of goodbye would have been nice.

Face it, she told herself, standing on the veranda and facing the stables and protective ring of trees, *you wanted to see him this morning. You were counting on seeing him this morning.*

It was true. All morning as she'd followed Señor Gutierrez around the stables she'd felt a bubble of excitement, a bubble she'd tried to suppress, but it had been there and she'd felt happy thinking she'd see Dante soon.

Now he was gone, and she had no idea when he'd be back.

The afternoon passed much more slowly, and Daisy was relieved when Señor Gutierrez sent her back to the house. Daisy had a solitary dinner before retiring to her room. It wasn't even nine when she turned out her light but she was tired and a little blue, and sleep offered a respite from thoughts of Dante.

A doorbell was ringing somewhere far away. Daisy was dreaming about Collingsworth Farm and didn't want to leave the dream behind. She pressed her pillow over her head, trying to block the doorbell, but it just rang and rang and finally she realized it wasn't the door, but the phone on her nightstand.

Rolling over, she lifted the receiver. *"Hola,"* she whispered groggily.

"Did I wake you, Daisy?"

Dante. She propped herself on her elbows. "What time is it?"

"Almost eleven. I didn't know you'd be in bed already or I would have waited for the morning."

"I was tired."

"I can call back—"

"No!" she interrupted, and then closed her eyes when she heard him laugh softly. He knew how she felt. Even if she pretended indifference, he knew better.

"I'm sorry about leaving so abruptly this morning. I made my meeting in Buenos Aires and then Anabella was being difficult. I meant to call earlier but the day got away from me."

"These things happen."

"You're hurt."

"I'm not hurt. I don't care—"

"You don't fool me with this 'I don't care' routine. You do care, Daisy. I care, too."

She pressed her forehead against her palm, squeezed her eyes shut and prayed for patience. "Let's not talk about this again. We're not getting anywhere and it just makes me crazy."

She heard him draw a slow breath.

"I think I'd like to see Daisy lose control," he said after a lengthy pause. "I think it would be incredible."

"Well, it's not going to happen."

"I wouldn't be so sure. We might just have to wait until you've returned to Kentucky, but it will happen. I promise you."

CHAPTER SEVEN

IF HE thought his promise was a comfort to her, he was wrong.

Daisy slugged her pillow hard and then again before finally getting comfortable and falling back asleep. But in the morning her temper was still on edge.

Thankfully, working with Señor Gutierrez helped keep her mind off Dante—during the day at least. At night, however, she found herself thinking about him endlessly. It was awful wanting someone this much, awful craving contact. She thought she'd give anything to be in his arms, against his chest, breathing him in.

She'd never felt like this before. If this was lust she could do without it.

Four days passed, four very long days. When she finished work on Thursday she remained at the paddock near the stable, not able to face returning to the empty hacienda-style house.

This is for the good of the family, she reminded herself, picking up the heavy rope and tying it into a loose knot. *You're here for Dad and Zoe, and it won't be forever.*

She swung the rope over her head and let it fly. The loop landed around a fence post and she pulled hard, cinching the knot.

"Do it again."

The voice was Dante's, the energy his, too. Daisy felt a shiver run through her. Slowly she turned and looked over her shoulder. He was every bit as tall and sexy and devilishly gorgeous as she remembered. "Hello, count."

Was that cool, calm voice hers? She couldn't believe she could sound so calm when her heart had begun to race, thumping like a wild bronc.

"Can you do it again?" he asked, leaning on the fence railing, watching her where she stood in the center of the ring.

"Of course. I could lasso you, if I wanted."

His eyes gleamed. "You're that good?"

"I'm very good."

His laugh, husky and low, soothed her somehow. "You've never lacked confidence."

He was wearing jeans and boots and a tight black T-shirt and as he swung himself up onto the top railing, muscles popped in his forearms and biceps.

She felt heat bloom within her, and happiness, too. She shouldn't care that he was back and yet everything in her was responding to him. Everything was turning on. "Why should I? I can do anything I want to do."

"I'll have to remember that." The way he said it sounded very sexual and lethal at the same time.

He watched her move to the fence post and untie the knot she'd thrown. He was a couple feet away but she felt him so strongly that her hands shook.

"Señor Gutierrez said you're a fast study," he said.

The sun was beginning to drop in the sky but it was still warm, still a beautiful day. The blue of the sky stretched forever. She stalked to the center of the ring. "I could have told you that."

"He said you know what you're doing."

"I think I did tell you that." Her lips twitched. "About a hundred times."

"Not a hundred," he answered mockingly. "Maybe eight times."

"Nine," she retorted.

"You are incredibly stubborn."

"Yes. One of my many virtues."

"You do have many virtues, but I don't think stubbornness is one of them."

"Maybe you just need to learn to appreciate it."

He laughed softly, and she cast him a cool glance. Their eyes met, and Daisy saw appreciation in his gaze, appreciation and something else that made her heart falter and her belly tighten.

He wanted her.

Her throat felt raspy as she breathed in. She forced her stiff fingers to get a better grip on the rope. Desire was something she didn't know how to deal with, especially since that desire had to take a back seat to everything else happening.

What good was desire then?

But she couldn't think this way, couldn't think of the wanting or the needing because it would only lead to disappointment. If she let herself start feeling she'd just get trampled. Men like Dante didn't make commitments. Anabella had virtually said the same thing. Men like Dante made love and walked away.

She hated the walking away part because she hated

being left behind. She could ride a horse, rope a steer, jump a fence, deliver a foal. But she couldn't say goodbye.

Yet she'd have to say goodbye. If not tomorrow, then in a few weeks. Her insides knotted. She twirled the rope higher overhead until she was standing beneath the spinning circle. "How long are you going to be back?"

"Just for the night."

Her heart plummeted to her toes in the tips of her boots. "What brought you back?"

"You."

She almost dropped the rope. The loop sagged and she caught the circle with her other hand. Turning to face him, she wiped a bead of moisture from her brow. "Me?"

"I need your help." He jumped off the fence into the center of the ring. "I was hoping you'd help me with Anabella for a few days until I can find her a suitable chaperone."

"A chaperone? But she's in school."

"She's already been kicked out. She's in her room right now, throwing a tantrum, I imagine."

That didn't take long, Daisy thought. "What happened?"

"The school wouldn't tolerate her promiscuous behavior." He said the word *promiscuous* as though it were a snake coiling on his tongue. "I don't believe she's actually promiscuous, but she's had a boyfriend, an unsuitable boyfriend, and she snuck out of the dorm to see him last night."

"Ah."

The furrow between his black brows deepened. "She's determined to ruin her reputation."

"She's seventeen."

"Not all girls are so bent on self-destruction."

"But not all girls are as intelligent as your sister. Anabella's very bright, Dante. She's going to push the limits." Daisy saw his perplexed expression and felt for him, she really did. Nothing could be more difficult than an emotional, hotheaded teenage girl. Daisy knew. She'd been one once. "Try not to worry," she added more gently. "She'll outgrow this stage."

"Not before I've lost my mind. She's running wild."

Daisy bent over to pick up the rope and begin coiling it together. "So leave her here with me."

"It'll be just for a few days, while I interview for a chaperone."

"No. Leave her here with me until you find a new school for her, and you go back to Buenos Aires and focus on your business." Daisy slung the coiled rope over her shoulder and braced her hands on her hips. Her long hair hung in a ponytail down her back, and tendrils clung to her warm cheeks. "You do have a corporation to run, don't you?"

He stared at her, his gaze fixed on a damp tendril clinging to her cheek. Daisy felt the warmth in his gaze, as well as the hunger he wouldn't act on. She didn't know whether to respect his willpower or resent it.

"She'll give you holy hell," he said at length.

"I'm not afraid."

"You're never afraid."

Only of my feelings for you.

But she didn't say it. The silence stretched between them. After an awkward moment she spoke. "Fair is fair. You've done plenty for me, this time I do a favor for you."

"I don't want a favor."

"I didn't, either, but you forced me to accept your help. You knew we needed it. You need help now." They both had pride, too much pride.

"I'll pay you to watch her, or I can reduce the interest."

"This isn't a business deal and I refuse to make it one."

He walked away, and taut with frustration, she threw the rope, lassoing the fence post. Bull's-eye. Of course. Too bad she couldn't manage her emotions as easily as the rope.

The next morning she walked with him to his car. She was lousy at goodbyes, hated goodbyes, and just wanted him to go—quickly.

"Daisy."

She couldn't look at him. Her heart was thudding wildly and her hands were shaking so hard she had to jam them into the pockets of her jeans.

She didn't want him to go and felt precariously close to begging him to touch her, just once. A hand to the cheek, a touch to the neck, something, anything. "When will you be back?" Her voice sounded husky even to her ears.

"So you will miss me."

"That's not what I said."

"But will you miss me?"

"No." *Liar, liar,* she silently chanted. Of course she'd miss him. She was already missing him.

"That's right. Daisy Collingsworth doesn't need anyone."

She flushed but didn't contradict him. He was right, in a way. She'd never needed anyone before. All her life she'd been taught to face problems head-on, to not make excuses and to not ask favors. "I can take care of myself."

Dante's hand hovered over the phone on his desk. He wanted to call her, wanted to hear Daisy's voice and the smart sassy things she liked to say to him. He wanted to feel her smile because he could always tell when she was smiling.

He lifted the receiver, started to bring it to his ear before replacing it in the cradle.

He couldn't call her. There was nothing to say. Well, he supposed he could ask about Anabella, but he'd asked yesterday and everything was fine.

If only he was fine. He felt terrible.

He'd thought that putting distance between himself and Daisy would help. It should have helped. Unfortunately it wasn't working that way with Daisy. She was far too tempting, far too smart and sexy and stubborn.

Dante smiled faintly. He must be out of his mind if he was beginning to find her stubborn streak appealing. He must be out of his mind to crave her like this.

Normally women didn't intrude into his personal life...at least, not beyond the bedroom. He'd learned to keep his wants and needs separate, dividing love from lust, but his attraction to Daisy was confusing the issue, confusing him.

Por dios, she had him in knots, and the rawness of his desire only deepened, a fire in his gut that burned all the way through him until he couldn't think of anything but her. He'd never wanted a woman as badly as he wanted Daisy.

At the airstrip when they'd first arrived, and when he'd kissed her, she'd felt impossibly right in his arms. Her body fit his, her mouth tasted sweeter than candy, and he wanted more. And the more he wanted her the more he mistrusted his desire.

He couldn't afford to lose his focus. He couldn't risk Anabella's stability or happiness.

Once he'd allowed his own interests to cloud his judgment, and the results had been devastating. While his younger brother, Tadeo, had self-destructed in Buenos Aires, Dante had embraced New York and his high-profile job on Wall Street. He had lived with a beautiful American blue blood in an expensive Third Avenue town house as though he had no ties, no obligations, no responsibilities but his own desires.

It wasn't until he'd stood at Tadeo's funeral that he'd faced the bitter truth. Dante had failed Tadeo. Just as their father had failed them.

Dante understood then that *his* needs must come second. They had to. It didn't mean that he didn't have needs, but he could prioritize, and he did. He couldn't bring Tadeo back, but he could ensure his sisters' well-being.

Now, three years later, Dante was sharply reminded of those priorities, particularly since his responsibility was cohabitating with his desire.

Roughly he lifted the phone again and dialed the *estancia*'s number. Daisy answered.

"How is Anabella?" he asked curtly. No hello, no how are you.

Daisy felt his anger. She didn't understand it, either. Everything was fine at the *estancia*. She and Anabella had been getting on very well, and Anabella had resumed her independent studies thanks to Daisy's supervision. "She's fine. She's out riding right now. I can have her call when she returns."

"Shouldn't you be riding with her?"

"Why? She's seventeen."

"And has a penchant for running away."

"She won't run away."

"How do you know? You just met her less than two weeks ago."

Daisy closed her eyes, tipped her head against her hand. What did he want from her?

"You have to watch Anabella closely," he added. "You can't trust her too much."

"I'm careful."

"And you'll call me if she does become a problem?"

"Yes. But we're fine. She's fine. I'm fine."

"That's what you always say."

His voice rasped, and she felt his frustration. "But isn't that what you want me to say?"

"Only if it's true."

"It is true. I grew up taking care of Zoe, and taking

care of Anabella isn't as difficult as you think. She's a great person. I enjoy her company quite a bit.''

He didn't speak for quite a long time. ''But who looks after you?''

She felt a lump swell in her throat. ''I don't need looking after.''

''Haven't you ever wanted someone to take care of you?''

''I'm not helpless. I can take care of myself.''

Again silence stretched over the phone line. Daisy felt his tension. It fairly vibrated through the phone. ''I'll be back Friday.''

''I know. And please don't worry, Anabella and I are managing just fine.''

Phone call over, Daisy gave herself a mental pat on the back. She and Anabella were doing fine, too.

In fact, Anabella had been on such good behavior that four days later, on Thursday, Daisy proposed an excursion.

''What would you like to do, Anabella? Go for a drive, out to lunch, maybe do some shopping?''

''All three,'' Anabella answered, pouncing happily on the idea. ''We can go to Santa Rosa. It's not too long a drive, and we can shop and have lunch there.''

Hours later, Daisy sat in the plaza restaurant, clasping her cup of café con leche and leaning back in her chair to savor the warm sunshine.

It had been a wonderful afternoon, just what they needed, and Daisy couldn't help congratulating herself for her brilliant suggestion. They'd shopped, enjoyed a wonderful meal and finally stopped for coffee at a bakery on the old town square.

The clock in the city hall tower chimed, and Daisy counted the hours. Half past four. As soon as Anabella returned from the washroom they'd need to head home.

Bill paid, sunglasses perched on the end of her nose, Daisy continued to wait for Anabella. But the minutes crept by without a sign of the teenager, and as fifteen minutes turned to twenty and twenty to twenty-five, Daisy felt dread.

Something was wrong. Anabella had been gone far too long.

Gathering their shopping bags, Daisy checked the women's washroom and found it deserted. She asked the bakery staff if they'd seen Anabella leave. No one knew anything. Heart in mouth, Daisy rushed to the car, but Anabella wasn't there either.

Daisy's dread turned to denial. How could this be happening? How could Anabella disappear? It was impossible. It hadn't happened. Daisy just wasn't thinking clearly.

Fishing the car keys from her purse, she climbed into the car and began driving the city streets, scouring the neighborhoods, searching the narrow cobbled alleys as well as the newer boulevards. But there was no sign of Anabella anywhere.

She'd have to call Dante.

Daisy's stomach cramped, filled with pins and needles. She couldn't even imagine how she'd break the news to him. He'd be livid. He'd blame her. And so he should.

She didn't have permission to leave the *estancia*. She hadn't watched Anabella closely enough, especially considering the girl's history of running away. Daisy had been lulled into complacency, and look what had happened—disaster.

But maybe Anabella hadn't run away. The girl was an heiress, incredibly beautiful; she might have been kidnapped...or worse.

Daisy shuddered at the thought and silently blasted herself for not being more careful, not being more aware. This was not supposed to happen. Temper, anger, nerves and fear wrestled for the upper hand. Daisy's hands shook on the steering wheel as she drove, and she chewed her lower lip, so sick at heart that the twenty-five miles back to the *estancia* felt like hours.

At last the private lane to the *estancia* came into view. Daisy switched on the blinker and signaled her turn. Driving onto the narrow road, she approached the alley of trees, and there, near the front of the trees in the shade, walked Anabella.

Daisy couldn't believe it. Trembling, she pulled the car to the side of the road, faced the startled Anabella and opened the passenger door. "Get in."

Daisy was so angry she could hardly see straight. Anabella's mascara formed smudged crescents beneath her eyes, and her lipstick was worn away. "What happened? Where were you?"

The girl shifted. "I went to the ladies' washroom but when I came back you were gone."

"I waited a half hour for you."

"I went to the—"

Daisy wasn't in the mood for this. "You left the bakery, you left me there, Anabella. Where did you go?"

"Nowhere. I told you—"

"Don't, Anabella, don't tell me another lie. I trusted you. And you know it, too." Seething, hands still shaking, Daisy shifted into drive and wordlessly drove them the rest of the way home.

Pulling in front of the house, Daisy spotted a luxury sedan parked off a ways, a slate-colored Mercedes gleaming in the early evening sun.

"Uh-oh," Anabella whispered, "Dante's home."

It was worse than uh-oh. Dante was furious. He'd come back a day early, eager to see his sister, and he'd been waiting nearly two hours for their return.

The moment Daisy turned off the ignition, Dante wrenched her door open. "Where were you?"

Words died on Daisy's tongue. She'd seen him angry, but this was something else. This wasn't just fury, it was worry, fear, insecurity.

Anabella jumped into his arms. "Did you miss me?"

He pushed her back. "You didn't have permission to leave the *estancia*." Then he turned on Daisy. "What were you thinking? You didn't have permission to take my sister off the ranch, and if you'd wanted to go, you should have called."

Daisy climbed out of the car. She couldn't argue with him, and after having just gone to hell and back with Anabella's disappearing act, she realized that it could have been much worse.

But he wasn't finished with her yet. "The housekeeper said you were gone for almost six hours. *Six hours*. Where were you?''

"Shopping," Anabella answered blithely. "Daisy took me to lunch in Santa Rosa and we did some shopping before stopping for a coffee. It was lovely. It was Daisy's idea, and we had an absolutely wonderful day."

Daisy's idea. How clever of Anabella. Set Daisy up so Daisy would feel too awkward, too guilty, to tell Dante about Anabella's escapade.

But Daisy knew what Anabella had done. She knew the girl had left the restaurant, gone somewhere with who knew whom, and—

Daisy couldn't even finish the thought, wondering how she could have possibly been so foolish as to think she could trust Anabella. She should have listened to Dante. He'd warned her. But Daisy thought she knew everything.

Her stomach burned. She felt like she'd swallowed acid. "I'm sorry. I was wrong."

"But we had fun," Anabella insisted, shooting Daisy a worried side glance. "Didn't we, Daisy? It was a great time, and I owe all my thanks to you."

"Anabella, you go to your room, I want a word with Daisy."

"Don't be mad at Daisy, we had such a good time—"

"Go," he interrupted harshly, pointing to the house. "And stay there until I come for you."

Anabella cast Daisy a pleading last glance before fleeing into the house.

Dante jammed his hands into his olive-green slacks, white shirt open at the collar, exposing his tan throat and the hard, taut planes of his chest. He looked too raw, too virile, and Daisy felt an inarticulate craving to touch him, unbutton his shirt and slide her hand across the tanned skin.

"You had no business taking her off the property." His voice was curt. "You should have called me, you should have asked permission."

"If you can't trust me, then fire me, or send me home or take some kind of action, because I'm sick and tired of words."

"This isn't about you and me."

"That's where you've got it wrong, Dante. This is totally about you and me. It's about you not trusting me and you not respecting me—"

"That's ridiculous."

"Call it what you want, but I'm not going to stand here and take another lecture from you. I'm doing my best. I'm sorry it's not enough. But maybe you expect too much out of people. You certainly want the impossible from me."

She walked away from him. She had to. Or she'd say something she'd regret....

CHAPTER EIGHT

DANTE followed her, chasing her to her bedroom. "I'm not finished."

"I am," she retorted, reaching for the door. Her wounded pride had had it. "Move. Before I slam the door on your head."

He stuck his foot in the door. "You're strong, Daisy, but you're not that strong."

"I don't need this. You left me in charge—"

"Correction, Daisy, I didn't leave you in charge. I left you here to watch over my sister, but watching over her is different from driving her about the country providing her with opportunities for disaster."

"Nothing happened." *No?* she silently mocked herself. *Something did happen, only you're too much a coward to tell him.*

"You're lucky then. Because Anabella has an amazing ability to sneak off and create utter chaos, and trust me, Ana doesn't need more chaos. She needs structure, order, discipline."

"I was with her—"

"That's not the point. You weren't supposed to be out. You weren't supposed to take the car."

"Stop talking to me like I'm fifteen."

"Then start acting like a grown-up!"

Her hands clenched, and she lifted one fist.

"Are you going to hit me again? Is this your way of dealing with problems?"

He was right. She was acting like a child.

Daisy dropped her hand, retreated into her room, her heart racing. She couldn't handle this, couldn't articulate how much his words hurt her. She wished she didn't care what he thought, wished she didn't care at all about him or his wretched arrogant opinion, but she did care. Cared deeply.

He'd destroyed her independence ages ago, but she didn't want to admit it. From their very first kiss she'd wanted more from him than she'd ever wanted from anyone. With one kiss she'd taken more chances, opened herself to more hurt, than she'd ever felt comfortable doing before.

And look where it had gotten her.

"I don't want to fight."

"Good, because you'd lose, and frankly, I don't have the time or energy to get into another arm-wrestling match. As smart as you are, and as independent as you like to think you are, you don't always know what's best."

Even as he spoke, he continued walking toward her, a slow, deliberate march that made the fine hair on her neck rise and her muscles tense.

Daisy backed up a step and then silently criticized herself for being a coward, but it was all she could do to hold her position when he stopped in front of her, less than a foot away. She could feel the heat of his body, and the width of his shoulders reduced her to something small and fragile.

"Tell me just one thing, and be honest."

She stiffened. "What?"

He reached out, lifted a long gold strand of hair and tucked it behind her ear. "Were you with Anabella every minute this afternoon? Did she leave you at any point? Disappear for awhile? Fifteen minutes? Twenty?"

Daisy held her breath. She felt his gaze search hers. She couldn't lie to him and she couldn't tear her gaze from his intensely erotic eyes. He looked so beautiful and he kissed like the devil and everything she felt had to be wrong. "I did lose her," she whispered. "In the market square this afternoon."

"How long was she gone?"

"Two hours. Give or take twenty minutes."

"You didn't suspect she'd sneak away?"

Daisy colored. "No." He was making her feel very stupid. "I generally don't mistrust people."

"But you continue to mistrust me." He reached out again, slipped a hand through her hair, letting the long, silvery strands drape across his fingers.

Her lips parted, but she couldn't really argue that point. He was right. She didn't trust him. Or maybe she didn't trust herself.

He tugged her hair and lifted her face to his. His smoldering gaze traveled her face, focusing first on her eyes and then her mouth. "You weren't going to tell me that you lost Anabella in town, were you?"

Her throat constricted. She couldn't speak and just shook her head.

"Why not? You didn't think I ought to know she's up to her old tricks? That she's sneaking behind my back, meeting her boyfriend again?" There was an edge to his voice.

"It's not as if you can change what's happened at this point."

"I can't change what happened this afternoon, but I can ensure it doesn't happen again. Her boyfriend is bad news. Very bad news, and Ana doesn't need to be exposed to more pain."

"Your intentions are good, Dante, but you can't possibly control her. You can give her guidance and support. You can offer encouragement, but in the end Anabella is responsible for Anabella."

"No. You don't understand—"

"I do, better than you think."

"I can't discuss this right now," he said curtly, his expression dark, frustration rolling off him in waves.

"You mean you won't."

"Exactly." He drew her against him, and his head suddenly dipped, his mouth covering hers.

As his lips touched hers, Daisy felt a wall of heat slam into her. It was huge, tangible, physical. Something happened when they touched, and it was bigger than either of them, stronger, more powerful.

He kissed her deeply, parting her lips with his, his tongue tasting her mouth before teasing her tongue in a slow, erotic dance. He was awakening every nerve and sense, creating a fierce hunger that could only, would only, be consummated by him.

Long minutes later, when he finally lifted his head, Daisy clung to him, dizzy, legs utterly boneless.

His breathing was labored, and he lifted her face, his savage gaze inspecting her languid expression and swollen lips.

"I want you, Daisy, and maybe there's a way we can make this work, but it won't happen if you fight me regarding Anabella."

Her heart continued to thud hard, her pulse racing. She wanted him desperately but she wouldn't play games with him. She had a mind, she had her own opinions, and he had to be willing to listen to her opinions. "I'm not going to fight with you about your sister but I don't have to agree with your point of view, either."

He gently but firmly pushed her away so that she felt only cool air surrounding her. "You're better off biting your tongue."

"I can't do that."

"Then maybe it's time you went home."

Daisy felt the blood drain from her face. She went cold all over, fingers, toes, legs. "Maybe it is." Unconsciously she lifted her chin, not about to crumble even though she was shocked. She'd never expected those words out of him.

Dante's gaze met hers, eyes narrowed, amber irises stormy. "We'll talk about this later. I don't have the time now. I have guests arriving at the airstrip within the hour."

"You have guests flying in?" For some reason her brain felt slow, her emotions clouding her thoughts. She should be pleased she could go home. She should be pleased she'd be back on her farm taking some control over her life again.

"A group of clients and business associates," he answered tautly, turning and looking toward the door. His jaw was tight, his lips compressed. "I thought things were going well here or I wouldn't have invited them for a long weekend. I frequently use the *estancia* to entertain and planned a traditional barbecue for tonight."

"I'll try to stay out of your way."

"That's not what I want." He shot her a swift glance, his eyes narrowed. "I wanted my guests to meet you. I thought you'd enjoy the party." His jaw softened somewhat. "I still think you would. I'll expect to see you and Anabella dressed by seven."

"I don't want to go, not the way I feel right now."

"They know you're here. It would be an embarrassment if you didn't show. I expect you dressed by seven. *Si?*"

Daisy felt trapped between Anabella's deceit and Dante's demands. For the first time since she arrived in Argentina she truly felt like an outsider and realized she might not be able to handle juggling responsibilities along with these new emotional demands.

Unable to find peace in her bedroom, Daisy changed into her jeans, boots and a light cotton pullover. She knew Dante expected her at the party but she was in no mood to help entertain his guests. If he wanted to host a party, let him host it.

Daisy had a horse saddled and brought to her, a young thoroughbred appropriately named Nino, or Baby. But Nino wasn't timid. She loved to run, and once they'd left the gates of the estate, Daisy leaned forward in the saddle and let the mare go.

Cantering across the pampas, hair streaming loose behind her, knees gripping the mare's sides, Daisy wouldn't let herself think of anything but the open land and the cooling evening breeze. She'd forget Anabella, forget Dante, forget the debt, her father's health, forget everything but the rare luxury of time alone.

In the lavender and silver twilight, her senses felt unusually heightened. She could smell the soil and the tender shoots of grass. The sky looked like pewter, and the distant line of trees darkened to purple.

Riding hard on an approaching fence, Daisy rose in the stirrups and encouraged Nino to jump. The mare obliged, and they sailed over the fence. Daisy hugged Nino's neck and they cantered on.

But an hour later the sun had completely disappeared. And she had no choice but turn back. Daisy took a different route home, following an old dirt road. About a mile from the house she approached another rider. He wore traditional pants and boots. He must be one of the *estancia*'s hired gauchos.

"Buenos noches," she said on reaching the cowboy.

He nodded. He was young, couldn't be much older than twenty-two or twenty-three, but he was tall and looked strong, as though he'd already spent a lifetime in the saddle. Yet he turned away from her smile, his heavy brows furrowing as though he didn't welcome the attention.

Perhaps he wasn't one of the hired hands after all.

Maybe he was one of those renegade gauchos Dante had told her about.

Daisy urged Nino faster and galloped the rest of the way home. Heart pounding, hands trembling, she stripped off Nino's saddle as soon as they reached the stable. She shouldn't have gone out so late in the day. No harm had come to her, but it was foolish to take unnecessary risks. She couldn't afford to take unnecessary risks, not when Zoe and her dad depended on her so much.

She'd mention the gaucho to Dante, let him know what she'd seen. Just in case, he ought to know.

As she left the stable, she heard music coming from the manicured lawn on the other side of the house and remembered Dante's get-together. From the sound of the laughter, the party was in full swing. Daisy moved quietly through the house and carefully opened her door, reaching into her room to snap on the light.

Dante's voice thundered from the shadows. "I've been looking everywhere for you."

She quickly flicked the light on. His piercing gaze traveled the length of her, grimly studying her damp, disheveled appearance. "Where have you been?"

"I went for a ride."

"You were supposed to join us for dinner."

He shattered what was left of her calm. All thoughts of the gaucho flew out of her mind. "This isn't my party, Dante, and those aren't my clients. You can ask Anabella to attend, but you can't make me."

"Not a good time for arguing, Daisy. I've held dinner for you. My guests are waiting on you. Get dressed."

She hated his tone and how helpless he made her feel. But she didn't back down when cornered, she came out swinging. "I have no intention of joining your clients tonight, so don't bother holding dinner a moment longer because I *won't* be joining you."

"Wrong. You will be joining me, even if I have to dress you myself," he said, swinging her into his arms.

He slung her against his chest. His cologne filled her nose, his warmth permeated her body, and she found herself responding to him, breasts swelling, nipples tightening, belly contracting. Then he dropped her on her bed, stepped back a step and glared at her. "For the last time, Daisy, I'm asking you to wash, dress and join my guests."

"And for the last time, I'm telling you no."

His hands moved, his instincts quick. With a flash he stripped her of her cotton pullover, leaving her in bra and jeans in the center of her bed. "Then I'll get you ready myself as I don't have energy for two rebellious teenagers." His hands jutted on his hips beneath the elegant cut of his dinner coat. "Make up your mind, Daisy, I'm out of patience."

She scrambled to her knees, fuming. "And just what am I supposed to wear?"

He stalked to her closet and threw the door open. "I swear, Daisy, you can be a bigger baby than my sister."

"And you, Dante lack tact, diplomacy, compassion—"

"Sensitivity, too, I've been told."

"Then work on it!" she shouted, grabbing the pillow

from her bed and flinging it at his back. It hit him high, between the shoulder blades. *Good hit, Daisy*.

He turned his head barely an inch. "Careful. Or I'll take your jeans off next."

She watched as he ruthlessly sorted through her hanging clothes, examining her meager wardrobe of skirts, blouses, sundresses, the metal hooks on the hangers scraping the wood pole, and winced at the parade of clothes, seeing it through his eyes.

"This is all you brought?" he drawled.

"It's all I own."

He glanced at his watch, noted the late hour and swore beneath his breath. "*Dios*, it's late. I'll have to find you something from my sister's closet."

"Anabella is half my size."

"Not Anabella's clothes, Estrella's. She still keeps some things here, and she's tall like you. I'm sure she has something that'll work."

Still warm and damp from a hurried bath, Daisy slid into a pair of lace underpants just as her bedroom door flung open. Dante was back.

She made an ineffective grab at her robe, and he snorted as if mocking her modesty. Blushing, she took the beaded black two-piece number from him and turned around to dress.

He waited outside the room while she dressed, but she needed his help to zip the tiny beaded tank top. Finally dressed, he escorted her out, but from his grim expression, she knew the evening would be a disaster.

The patio tables had been set with linens and fresh

flowers. Candles flickered on the tables, and the musicians played, plucking softly at the guitars.

During dinner Daisy sat with Anabella at a table opposite Dante's. Anabella fidgeted restlessly and barely ate any of the barbecue. "Are you okay, Ana?" Daisy asked, concerned.

"*Si, si,*" the girl answered, managing a small smile, but the smile didn't reach her eyes.

Daisy felt Dante's gaze on her, and she struggled to ignore him. She succeeded once, but when he focused on her again ten minutes later, she felt weak on the inside. Quivery.

She didn't know how it happened or when it happened, but he'd changed her life, become part of it. Whether she stayed in Argentina or returned to Kentucky, she'd be different.

After dinner the musicians played again, a sultry tango that had the guests taking to the dance floor with good-natured laughter.

Dante danced with a couple of the women who were visiting, and Daisy tried not to watch, finding it too painful to see another woman in his arms.

This was wrong, she thought, increasingly distraught. She was feeling too much, wanting too much, taking him too seriously. He'd never promised her anything but financial help, and even that was structured into a contract for the farm. She couldn't want more from him because she wasn't going to get more.

But her stern reminder didn't work. It didn't fill the hollow feeling inside of her, and it didn't soothe her heart. She left her chair, moved to the corner of the patio to get a glass of water. The water tasted cold but it only emphasized her numbness, enforced her internal chill. She felt lost and incredibly confused. She felt most unlike herself, most unlike the Daisy she let the world see.

Eyes burning, throat hurting, she took another sip of the ice water.

A hand lightly touched her shoulder. "Dance with me, Daisy."

That voice belonged to only one man, the man she wanted more than anyone else in the world. Unable to speak, she turned to face him, her gaze riveted to his face. "I don't think I can."

"It's easy. Just touch me."

He took her hand, drew her out to the dance floor and brought her into his arms. It was like coming home, she thought, eyes closing, cheek nestling against his chest. She was exactly where she wanted to be.

The song was slow, and they danced slowly. Daisy forgot everyone, too intent on savoring the moment, remembering the glorious sensation of being in his arms, against his heart.

Her long loose hair brushed the middle of her bare back. His hand cupped her low on her spine, fingertips against the curve of her derriere. After awhile she couldn't feel the floor or hear the music, her senses too attuned to his hand on her and her internal response, her body turning on for him, melting into liquid heat.

Dante turned his head, kissed the inside of her bare upper arm. She shuddered and knew he could feel it.

"Maybe we should stop dancing," she said, feeling naked with need, fearful her control would soon shatter.

"You really want to stop?"

"We should, shouldn't we?"

"Are you asking me?"

She felt like honey, inside and out. His mouth brushed her bare shoulder, the side of her neck. Half closing her eyes, she gave way to the bittersweet sensation, hot and cold, sharp and creamy, everything intensely sensitive.

Daisy slid her hands across his shoulders, feeling the heat of his hard, muscled body through his elegant dinner jacket. She pressed herself closer, knees quivering, body throbbing. She couldn't stand much longer without his support. How could she want him like this?

Suddenly he was pulling her after him, away from the crowded dance floor, into the house, down a dim hallway to his darkened study.

"*You've* done this to me," he whispered, shutting the door behind them. "I can't get enough of you."

CHAPTER NINE

HE PRESSED her against the door frame and stepped boldly between her thighs, drawing the black silk skirt taut against her bottom. He took another step between her thighs, widening them, making room for his hard, aroused body.

Dante's mouth crushed hers. He opened her lips with his tongue, raking the sensitive contours of her mouth, thrusting at the hollow beneath her cheek, even tracing the roof of her mouth.

Trembling from head to toe, she clung to him, clasping his arms for support. She felt mindless with wanting and opened her mouth wider to him, her tongue finding his, teasing back.

He groaned deep in his throat, and she felt a flare of triumph. *He wanted her!*

She slid her hands from his shoulders to his chest, caressing the broad plane of muscle and down to his flat abdomen, feeling the muscles tighten, lengthen at the quest of her hand.

His hips ground against hers, his erection creating friction and fresh desire. She'd never felt so primitive in her life, and she raked her nails over his white dress shirt, scratching at his chest, wanting skin instead of polished cotton.

"You're driving me wild." He gritted the words, dragging his hand up her thigh, hiking her skirt up, bringing the flimsy silk around her hips.

As his fingers slid beneath the lacy edge of her panties she sighed, fingers twisting in his shirt, holding tight as his fingers explored the soft skin of her inner thigh.

Daisy wanted him in her, wanted to make love right here against the door, even with the music and voices blaring outside. Somehow in the crush of clothing and with the heady scent of his cologne flooding her senses she knew this was exactly right, this was how it should be. Intense, real, consuming.

Her arms wrapped around his neck, and she pulled his head closer, tasting his mouth, drinking him in and the play of her lips drew an immediate and ardent response from him. His palm cupped her and his fingers found her moist heat. She sucked in air.

"Preciosa," he murmured against her mouth, his voice husky, hungry. "I want you."

She helped unbuckle his belt, frantically worked his zipper down. She wanted to touch him, wanted to make him feel half as good as he was making her feel.

Sliding her hand around him, she discovered he was already long and thick, yet as she stroked him, he grew. Her delight was matched by awe and even a bit of fear.

He kissed her mouth, her upper lip and the curve of her cheek. "We'll go slow. Just enjoy, yes?"

"Yes." She murmured agreement, feeling shy as he lifted her, wrapped her legs around his bare waist.

The heat of his hands against her bare bottom, the strength of his body as he supported her hips, the incredible sensation of his erection pressing at her most sensitive skin made her feel daring and dangerous. This was all so new and yet it felt so right.

She wanted to try everything with him, and as his body strained against hers, she shuddered, excited, nervous, curious. But Dante didn't rush, not at all. He simply held her against him, let her body get used to him, made sure she was as ready and hungry as he was.

Wonderful, her brain flashed, this was wonderful and he felt incredible, but she wanted more. With a wiggle, she brought herself down on him and continued to sink lower, accepting his fullness until she was completely connected to him.

He filled her, and Daisy drew a deep, shuddering breath, heat sweeping through her in red-hot waves. The fusion of their bodies was more intense than anything she'd ever experienced. She arched against him, breasts pressed to his chest, fingers gripping his shoulders.

As he began to move inside her, she felt new muscles tighten, inner muscles grip at him, hold him, want more of him. She felt wild and fierce, and each thrust of his hips made her cling tighter, each surge adding a layer of pleasure over the other. It was as though they were climbing a staircase, wrapped in each other, heading toward an impossible view.

Heart pounding, nerve endings screaming, she felt as though her senses were narrowing, focusing, fixing on something beautiful and overwhelming.

"Protection," Dante muttered, his mouth grazing hers. "I forgot protection."

Protection?

But it was too late for that, too late for thought or decision-making. She'd reached that high stair and she was tumbling down, caught up in the urgency and intensity of her first orgasm.

He came with her then, his body tightening, tensing before releasing into her.

It was amazing. No, more than amazing, it had been powerful, beautiful, stunning. This could become, she thought, kissing his mouth gently, completely addictive. She kissed him again and then the side of his neck. "Thank you."

"The pleasure's all mine."

Daisy gazed into his shadowed face. The words were right but the tone was wrong.

She tried to disengage, her sense of comfort fading as she felt his detachment. It was as though she were standing outside them, watching. She could see the ridiculousness of their position. Her panties on the floor. Her legs wrapped around his waist.

"Maybe I should get down," she said, clinging to whatever dignity she had left.

He didn't move immediately, and she pressed her palms against his thickly muscled shoulders to demonstrate her resolve. "Dante, put me down."

He placed her on her feet, and she scrambled to pick up her underwear and get it back on before smoothing her beaded skirt.

"I don't know what I was thinking." His voice was filled with self-loathing.

"I guess we weren't thinking."

"We should have been." His voice whipped at her.

"I should have been. I've never forgotten a condom before. I've never been so out of control."

"I'm sorry—"

"You could get pregnant."

She winced and bit down, humiliated. She felt stupid. Worse than stupid. Her eyes burned as she struggled to shake out the wrinkles in the skirt.

"You could get pregnant," he repeated, obviously wanting something from her.

She'd heard him the first time, she thought sickly. "There's a very slim chance, but yes, I suppose I could."

"I don't need that."

He was taking her heart and mashing it up, making her feel hateful and small. "Do you only think of yourself?" she asked, feeling a hot prickle in the back of her eyes. *Don't let me cry, please don't cry in front of him!*

"Don't be so sensitive. This isn't about you."

"Of course it's about me. It's my body!"

"But the baby would be my responsibility."

She burned hot and cold, and her fingers convulsively opened and shut. "If I was pregnant, I wouldn't need your help. I don't want your help, either."

"Awfully bold words from a woman who owes me a good chunk of change."

She felt wild, fiercely disorganized. "Life isn't only about money, Dante. It's about love, and if I did end up pregnant I'd have the baby and I'd love the baby and I'd be very happy, no thanks to you."

They were interrupted by the sound of raised voices and footsteps running through the house.

"Count Galván!" a voice cried in alarm. "Count Galván, where are you?"

Breathing hard, chest rising and falling, Dante stared at Daisy. "It's not personal, Daisy, so don't take this the wrong way, but I've no desire to get married and no desire to start a family. If I wanted a family I would have had one by now."

This was getting really painful. "I understand," she answered, her pride at an all-time low.

The voice was still shouting outside. "Count Galván!"

He continued to ignore the shout in the hall. "I have obligations," he said. "I'm committed to issues already."

"You don't need to say another word. I understand."

"I don't think you do."

"Just open the door," she said, hating the knot forming in her throat, hating the tangle of her emotions.

Mouth tight, eyes narrowed, he finished tucking his shirt in his trousers and buckled his belt. Leaning forward, Dante combed her long straight hair from her eyes and kissed her on her forehead.

"I'm sorry, Daisy."

She clasped the front of his shirt for a split second, inhaling his fragrance and his heat. Then she released him and stepped away. "Open the door. You're needed out there."

She was the one who yanked the door open. The harried cook who'd been running down the hallway stumbled to a stop.

"Anabella," the cook panted, face flushed, temples

beaded with perspiration, "is gone. No one has seen her for the past hour, and I overheard one of the hired hands say he saw her leave, and that she was carrying a small bag."

Dante turned ashen. "Gone?"

"Yes, with a bag. A little suitcase."

Dante didn't wait to hear more. He grabbed the car keys from his desk and raced outside.

Daisy followed him, arms crossed over her chest, chilled by the sudden turn of events. "What are you going to do, Dante?"

"Look for her. She can't be far."

"She's been gone at least an hour. Where are you going to look? Where will you go?"

He shrugged and slid behind the steering wheel. "I'll go to Santa Rosa and start there."

"And then what?"

"I'll bring her home. Keep her safe."

"Safe? You mean a prisoner?"

"Now you're starting to sound like Anabella! Come with me and help me look or stay behind, but don't try to stop me."

"I don't want to stop you, I'm just trying to understand what you hope to achieve by chasing after her and dragging her back."

"Anabella is seventeen!"

"She'll be eighteen in less than a month and soon a legal adult. You can't control her forever and you can't make choices for her, either—"

"I can surely try," he interrupted bitterly, starting the

car and slamming the door shut. "Especially if it'll save her life!"

Dante had called the police before leaving. The local detectives arrived at the *estancia* before Dante had returned home.

While waiting for Dante, a detective interviewed one of the ranch hands who claimed to have seen Anabella leave. The elderly gaucho admitted his eyes weren't so good anymore but he was certain that someone was waiting for Señorita Galván at the end of the driveway and it was a man on a horse.

Daisy's Spanish had improved since her visit but even then, she only understood part of the conversation. She did, however, catch the words man and horse, and she stiffened in horror. The man she'd seen earlier in the evening, the gaucho on the horse…

The detective heard her swift inhale. "What do you know?" he asked her.

What did she know? She'd seen a poor-looking gaucho on horseback. She'd seen him about a half mile from the *estancia*. He'd barely made eye contact with her.

Surely there were plenty of gauchos on the pampas. And just because she'd seen one gaucho on the road didn't mean that he was the man the elderly ranch hand had seen.

Sometimes she felt a little too world-weary, as though she'd seen more than her share of life at too young an age. Should she be more suspicious? More frightened? "I'm not sure I know anything," Daisy confessed. "I did see someone earlier on the road. But he was riding away from the *estancia*, not toward it, and that was several hours ago.''

The detective's eyebrows rose, and he scribbled something in his notebook. ''Doesn't sound like a kidnapping,'' he admitted. ''But since this is Señorita Galván, we owe it to the count to do a thorough investigation.''

By midnight, the house lights were half extinguished, the band packed up, and Dante's dinner guests hurriedly driven back to Buenos Aires. It was an awkward end to a party, and Daisy knew it.

The detectives were leaving when Dante returned home. One detective shared with Dante what he'd concluded. Anabella hadn't slipped away on the spur of the moment. The detective pointed out that the girl's purse and wallet were gone, her toothbrush, hairbrush and cosmetics. Shoes were missing from Anabella's closet and her warmest coat, too. Even the cash jar in the kitchen had been emptied, and left in the place of the cash was a note signed by Anabella reading IOU.

Dante held the note from the kitchen cash jar and stared at Anabella's girlish handwriting. ''So what happens now?''

Daisy heard the worry in his voice and felt his concern. He wasn't angry as much as heartsick. In his black dinner jacket, he looked big, fierce, intimidating. He could have been an avenging angel determined to retrieve his baby sister.

''Not a lot happens now,'' replied the detective. ''We'll put out a report, look for her in favorite haunts of runaways, but her birthday is coming up and if she's eighteen and wants to go—'' He shrugged. ''Then she can go where she wants. Disappear if she wants. That's her prerogative."

"But she's not eighteen yet, and we don't know that she's all right. We don't know that she wasn't taken against her will."

"I found no signs of a struggle."

"He might have knocked her out. And this man, this gaucho, might be holding her for a ransom."

"If that's the case, if you're contacted, call me immediately. I will be working at my desk all night. Tomorrow we will create a task force but I'm going to be honest, Count Galván, this is a big country with lots of open space. If she wants to lose herself…"

Daisy watched Dante where he stood at the large multipaned window in the living room, looking out into darkness. It was late, nearly one-thirty in the morning, and she knew he had to be as exhausted as she.

Silently she moved to the elegant sideboard and poured a brandy into one of the crystal snifters on the silver tray and carried the glass to him.

"She's a fool," he said grimly.

"She's young."

"And *foolish*."

Daisy felt incredible sympathy for Dante and his sister. They had such a complicated relationship, so much more difficult than her relationship with Zoe. "Part of growing up is experimenting, making mistakes. Anabella has to be allowed to make her fair share—"

"No!" His voice thundered. "My brother, Tadeo, was still a kid, just eighteen, and he wanted to experiment, too. Well, he ended up dying from experimenting." The anger and pain in Dante's voice washed over her in scalding waves. "Maybe some people would say that's part of life—and that there are always risks. But I don't agree, and I refuse to pay the same price twice."

She didn't know what to say. There was nothing she could say.

He took a sip from the glass, swirled the brandy and swallowed. "Ana's an aristocrat, worth a fortune, but when word leaks out that she's run away with a common cowboy, she'll be ruined. Among people I know in Buenos Aires, a mistake like this is never forgotten. A young woman with a tarnished reputation is worth nothing."

Daisy sat down on the edge of an upholstered chair. "What if she loves him?"

"Loves him? Loves whom? The gaucho?" His low laughter mocked her. "Daisy, you're so American."

She tensed. "Is that a problem?"

"It's not, if you're in America. But here, class matters. Class is everything. She cannot love a gaucho. She cannot marry a gaucho. Period. End of story."

"But you don't feel that way."

"No?"

Something in his voice filled her with foreboding. It was his tone, his attitude. Surely, she'd misunderstood him. "Dante, I'm middle class. I'm not part of the aristocracy, yet you made love with me."

"That's different."

She didn't want to ask, didn't want to know but couldn't stop herself. "How?"

"There are different kinds of women. Lovers." He hesitated. "And wives."

Of course he'd made her his lover. "What if one wants more? Can't one—" she couldn't bring herself to say *I* "—can't one be both?"

He looked down on her, deep grooves paralleling his sensual mouth. "Not in Argentina."

So he would make love to her but not marry her. He'd take her body but not keep her. It was almost too much on top of everything else that had happened that day.

He noticed her expression, must have read her hurt. He crossed the carpet, touched the back of her head, slid his fingers through her hair. "Don't make this about us. It's not about us. It's about Anabella."

She couldn't look at him. "But what about us? What about…what happened earlier?"

"I enjoyed it. I wanted you. Except the part where I forgot protection, I have no regrets." His hand coiled her hair, his fingertips brushing her bare nape. "And you? Are you regretting making love with me?"

She didn't regret it, but making love had complicated it even more. It had been difficult enough wanting him, but now that she knew the pleasure she'd find in his arms, it was impossible to forget it. It had felt so good. So right. And yet it was also so temporary. "No," she whispered, feeling betrayed, as much by herself as by him.

He wanted her to spend the night in his room, in his bed, and as much as he'd hurt her with his words, she still wanted to be with him because this—being together—wasn't going to last.

She'd never faced it before, hadn't even faced her feelings until now. She'd tried to pretend that it was surface, all action, almost like a sport. But it wasn't action and sport. It was all emotion. This was her heart.

She'd fallen in love with him.

It wasn't how she'd imagined love to feel. She'd thought love would be warm, cozy, comforting. But what she felt burned inside her, hot and livid and raw.

She hurt. Deeply, terribly.

For the first time since her mother died, Daisy cried.

She lay at the edge of Dante's massive sleigh bed, buried her face in the crook of her arm and curled into a ball. Her wet tears streaked her arm, and her mouth quivered as the sobs rose, her body shaking in an effort to control them.

She shouldn't cry now. She should have cried for her father's health, for her sister's distress, for the farm. She shouldn't cry over a man, and she especially shouldn't cry over Dante.

He wasn't worth it.

But the moment he reached out and touched her back, his hand sliding up to cup the back of her head, her heart squeezed so tight she thought it would break.

"Daisy," he murmured thickly, his voice husky with sleep. "Why are you crying?"

"I'm not," she croaked, trying to hate him, trying to gather her strength to get out of his bed and go back to hers, but she didn't move. She simply lay there wanting him, wanting more from him, wanting a future happiness she'd never considered until now but suddenly knew she couldn't live without.

His palm brushed her hair from her damp cheek, fingers untangling wet tendrils from her mouth and tucking each strand behind her ear. "I shouldn't have made love to you. I've been selfish. I've taken advantage of you."

"Because now that we've made love, I'm...cheap?"

Groaning, he dragged her from her corner into the center of the bed and into his strong arms. "No. You're not cheap. I never said that."

"But I've lost my value. You said a woman is a lover or a wife, not both."

His warm lips brushed her forehead, her temple and her tear-streaked cheek. "I could only make you my lover. It's my only choice."

If he thought he was helping, he was wrong, she thought, holding her breath, holding the air and the pain and the heartbreak in. Why hadn't she realized how she felt about him earlier? Why hadn't she known that all the physical things—the crazy racing pulse, the dizziness, the somersaults in her tummy—weren't just lust? Why didn't she know that love and lust could be identical things?

His lips covered hers lightly, fleetingly, and she tasted the salt of her tears on his mouth. "I still want you," he said softly. "I still want to love you."

As in, love my body.

A small broken cry escaped from her, and she pressed a fist against her mouth as if to keep the rest of the pain bottled inside.

"Daisy, don't do that. Look at me." He kissed her knuckles, the back of her fist, the bend in her wrist.

"This isn't like you. You're too smart and strong for this, and far too independent."

"Is that what you think?" she whispered, feeling fresh tears well, and her heart fall apart, a mashed-up plum inside her chest.

"It's what I know."

It wasn't fair, she silently raged, the hot tears brimming over yet again. She'd been strong for so many years, and yet what good had it done? How had it helped her?

Being strong was a curse.

"I have to go." She slid out from beneath his arm and scooted her legs over the bed. "Besides, we should call the police, check on Anabella."

"It's four in the morning, and the detective said he'd call if there's news."

"I know you're worried about her."

"Yes, but I can worry a little about you, too, can't I?"

She pushed her hair from her eyes, her cheek still damp with tears. "I shouldn't stay, though. It'll hurt to stay."

He made a hoarse sound in the back of his throat. "It can't hurt that much. I won't let it." He drew her back to him and rolled over her, settling between her thighs and covering her body with his.

He felt warm, hard, strong. And incredibly ruthless.

She was fighting for her heart, and he was winning.

Just before his mouth covered hers, she'd expected tenderness, but the moment their lips met, a hot current shot through her, sharp, intense, brilliant.

They made love with more passion than ever, loved fiercely, convulsively as though knowing their relationship had run its course and would very soon end. Daisy held him through the shuddering pleasure, and yet after the release, she found no peace inside her. This time making love only made the emptiness worse.

The early morning sun shone from behind the closed curtains, yellow light spilling at the edges and over the top. Dante woke first, and rising on his elbow gazed down at Daisy.

Last night had been intense, not just sexually, but emotionally.

When they made love he felt closer to her than he'd felt to anyone, and when she came, it gave him more pleasure than his own orgasm. They fit together. They made sense together. There was no reason for them not to be together.

If she could be content as his lover.

Gently he lifted a long silver strand from her neck and placed it with the shimmering mass on the pillow. He loved to look at her, loved the shape of her, loved the feel of her.

He'd always take care of her. She'd never want for anything. Clothes, house, car, cash, jewelry. She could travel, entertain and start a stable, anything—

Except take his name, and have his children.

What if she were pregnant now? Dante had used protection this last time. But what if last night, in his office, they'd made a baby?

She stirred, turned onto her back. He touched her pink cheek and then her parted lips. Her eyes slowly opened.

"Good morning," she whispered, and he stared in fascination at the pulse beating at the base of her throat, the pulse delicate beneath her skin, like the flutter of a butterfly wing.

"Good morning," he answered, his voice rough. He suddenly ached knowing he couldn't give her, wouldn't give her, what she wanted, much less what she deserved.

She touched him lightly on the chest, fingers resting just above his heart, the warmth of her touch burning all the way through him. Her lips struggled to curve, a small painful smile. "So what do we do now?"

Ravish you, he thought, his gut wrenching, his chest hard, tight. He wanted her and he wanted to keep her, but he couldn't promise fidelity, marriage or family. Her lips quivered beneath the caress of his thumb. "Please don't cry again, *muneca*."

"I won't." But her hand pressed into the muscle curving across his chest, nails sharp against the skin. He felt her struggle.

How had it all changed? Why had it changed?

Anabella.

He couldn't be all things to all people, and his family came first. Anabella had to come first. Certainly Tadeo hadn't, and look what happened.

But he didn't want to think about Tadeo or Anabella right now. He just wanted to hold Daisy, be with Daisy and enjoy the little time they had left.

Dante lowered himself, stretching out next to her, rib to rib, hip to hip. He kissed the corners of her mouth, savoring the soft warmth of her lips and the seductive texture of her skin. "Let's not make any decisions now."

"They'll have to be made eventually."

"Yes," he agreed with another slow, deep kiss. "But we have time."

CHAPTER TEN

A KNOCK sounded discreetly on the door, and the housemaid announced that the count had a call from the city. The caller insisted it was urgent.

Dante climbed naked from the bed, his tall muscular frame absolutely gorgeous in its maleness. Daisy watched as he stepped into briefs and slacks.

A half hour passed, and Dante didn't return. Daisy returned to her room, bathed and dressed. Venturing into the dining room, she found the table set for only one, her place. The count, she was told, took his breakfast this morning in his office.

Daisy was finishing her breakfast when Dante appeared. He'd showered and dressed since she last saw him, his nearly black hair crisp and combed, his bronze jaw cleanly shaven. With his polo-style shirt open at the collar he looked remarkably fit. And happier.

He knew something, she thought, something about Anabella.

"We're going to the city," he said, leaning over her, kissing her cheek.

He smelled heavenly, warm, spicy, rich. "*We* are?"

"Yes. As soon as you're ready."

They drove instead of flying to Buenos Aires, and Dante was in a remarkably buoyant mood, which again made Daisy question the phone call he'd received that morning and worry about its significance. What might be good for Dante might be disastrous for Anabella.

But she couldn't broach the subject with him. She knew already that he didn't welcome her thoughts on Anabella's future and freedom.

Caught up in the outskirts of Buenos Aires traffic, they slowed to a crawl. Dante popped in a jazz CD and rolled down the window. "I love the city," he said. "So much energy. So many possibilities."

She smiled faintly and forced her mind away from worry, reminding herself that above all Dante was a loving and devoted brother.

He smiled at her, white teeth flashing. "I'm glad you're here with me. We should have come to the city before. Made a trip in for dinner, dancing—" his eyes narrowed, lashes lowering as his gaze swept her "—pleasure."

Heat stole through her. She knew exactly what he meant by pleasure. After all, he'd spent some of the last twenty-four hours teaching her the definition of the word.

They dined that night at a spectacular restaurant in the heart of Recoleta, which was the name for his fashionable neighborhood. The restaurant was French, situated in the Alvear Palace Hotel, with a sister restaurant in Uruguay.

Daisy immediately loved the restaurant's pastel shades, deep plush chairs and the profusion of fresh flowers and pink candles everywhere. It was like a fairy tale, she thought, and yet amidst all this beauty and elegance, no one was more gorgeous than Dante.

He'd worn a black shirt and coat to dinner since the restaurant was very formal. But he didn't look morbid in all that black, he looked sinful. Like a man who knew all about love and sex and passion.

Despite the tempting menu, Daisy couldn't eat. She just wanted to go home and unbutton Dante's black silk shirt and touch his chest and make love, *now*.

She hated it, but she couldn't stop projecting into the future, couldn't stop anticipating what would happen, if not tomorrow, then soon.

She knew it was just a matter of time before he'd be with someone else, someone more appropriate, someone of his background, his class.

Daisy sat, tension growing inside her as she pictured him doing everything he was doing for her for another woman. She could see him fill her wineglass, see him lean in to hear her laughter, see him reach beneath the table to touch her thigh.

"Daisy." She jerked, gazed at him.

He stretched a hand across the table and touched her ear, her cheek. "Don't think about the future. The future isn't even here yet."

It was on the tip of her tongue to deny her worries, but in the end she simply shook her head once, a slow surrender, accepting the fact that she couldn't continue with this charade. "I have to go home."

"To my house?"

He knew what she meant, she thought with a pang, but he was determined to stick with the rules, continue playing the game. "Home to Lexington." She searched his eyes, looked for his true feelings. Perhaps there was more here. Perhaps there could be more.

"You really want a long-distance affair?"

"I don't want an affair."

"I can take care of you."

"I don't want you to take care of me, either."

Dante's eyes narrowed. "Then what do you want?"

"You know the answer already."

"Humor me, Daisy, especially if this is our last night together."

How awful it sounded! How bleak and lonely. Her lips trembled, but she forced herself to answer. "I want love. And I want respect."

Dante pushed aside the wineglass and wine bottle. "You don't think I respect you?"

The waiter glanced at their table as he passed by, concern evident in his expression. Their voices had begun to rise. Other patrons were taking notice.

"How do I not respect you?" Dante persisted. "I listen to you, I considered your feelings, I accept your suggestions. What am I not doing? How am I disrespecting you?"

His words flew at her, insistent and demanding. She swallowed hard, battling for courage. She lowered her voice. "First, you haven't accepted my suggestions and you don't really listen to me. When I try to talk to you about Anabella—"

"That's different," he interrupted. "I'm talking about you and me."

"All right, you don't respect me enough to consider marrying me."

"We hardly know each other."

"Dante, don't be obtuse. You know me enough to want me. You know me enough to bring me halfway around the world, invite me to stay in your home and allow me to watch your sister. You know me."

"But my feelings on marriage have nothing to do with you."

"How can you say that with a straight face?"

"Daisy, please."

"Is there a law against marrying someone like me?"

"Not a written law, no."

"Just your culture. And your class."

"Why are you doing this here, and now?"

She didn't know why, but she couldn't leave it alone. She had to talk about it even if it meant destroying whatever was left between them.

She leaned across the table, hands outstretched. "I don't even know that I want to marry you, but the fact that you'd never consider me wife material makes me crazy."

He threw down his napkin. "You're making me crazy, too. You've known all along why you were here and what the agreement was."

"We're back to the contract." The debt. She'd always be in his debt. Of course. How could she forget? Daisy stood up, reached for her slim purse. "I'm going home. I'm going to pack and catch a plane back to Kentucky."

Dante stood, pressed her back into the seat. "The bill's not paid."

Her hands gripped her purse, knuckles white. She felt dead on the inside. "I don't want you to go with me. I'd rather return home and pack without you there."

"You might feel that way, but you won't walk out on me in the middle of a public place."

He didn't care about her feelings. It was just his pride. Saving face.

Daisy was grateful for the chair under her because she needed it. She couldn't have walked out at that moment even if she wanted to.

Dante signaled for the check, paid, and they headed outside. They didn't speak until they were in the back of his limousine.

"You created quite a show in there," he said flatly, stretching an arm out on the seat as he turned to look at her. "Did you accomplish what you wanted?"

She shuddered, appalled by the chasm yawning between them. "Don't blame all this on me. You're angry because I want more than casual sex."

"And when has this—us—ever just been casual? From the first time we met there were sparks, interest, awareness. We didn't just dive into casual sex. I've lost plenty of sleep over you, wondering how to best protect you, how to best take care of you—"

"Then talk to me, and I'll tell you what I need, but don't make decisions for me, and don't be so presumptuous as to assign me the mistress role!"

"You might not like it, but you are my lover, my mistress, my woman, whatever word you want to use. And it wasn't a problem last night when we finally made love. Why is it a problem now?"

"Maybe because I didn't know this was a dead-end relationship."

"I resent that, Daisy, but I'll let it go because we're both tired and it's been a long week. But before you start throwing accusations around, let me remind you that marriage was never an option from the start of things and it will never be an option. You knew that anything which developed between us was just a bonus, a gift—"

"Can you please not make it sound so much like a financial transaction?"

"Por dios!" He cursed beneath his breath, his body rigid with anger. "You're taking my words and twisting the meaning. My English is good, but you're making it inadequate."

She bowed her head and closed her eyes, the fight leaving her, the energy gone. She should have known this was a lost cause. How could she think she'd change him? "I'm sorry," she said softly, unable to continue arguing, not wanting to leave when there was so much distance and ice between them.

His sigh echoed her exhaustion. "Daisy, I don't like fighting with you."

"That makes two of us."

Suddenly he scooped her into his arms and settled her on his lap. "Good. We agree on something."

His warmth would be her undoing, she thought, pressing her cheek to his shoulder. In his arms she could never tell him no.

"I've been through hell with my family, Daisy." His voice had dropped and the tone was husky. "My father couldn't be faithful. He couldn't commit. Not to my mother, not to my stepmother, not to anyone. And we, his family, have paid a terrible price. I'm still trying to take care of the others, and I'm tired. I can't imagine taking on more pressure, more obligations, more family."

"You don't want children? No heirs to carry on the Galván name?"

"And curse them with the Galván history? No. I wouldn't wish my blood on anyone." He kissed the top of her head and held her closer. "This shouldn't be so difficult, Daisy. It doesn't have to be difficult. I want to be with you. I love being with you. Can't that be enough?"

"And where will I live?"

"Here, in my house, or I'll get you your own place. Whatever you want."

"But there'll be no promises, no commitments. Is that right?"

"I can't offer marriage, no."

And he'd already said he didn't want kids. No marriage. No family. But she could have a house of her own.

Daisy had never heard of a worse deal in her life. No wonder the Galváns had earned such a terrible reputation. They took no prisoners in their negotiations.

She shifted in his arms to better see him. His face looked fierce in the flickering light as they passed beneath streetlight after streetlight. Helplessly she reached out to feel his nose, his chin, his chiseled jaw. "You'd make beautiful children, Dante."

He caught her fingers in his hand. "I don't want them,

Daisy. Trust me." He turned her fingers over and kissed them. "But I do want you."

"But for how long? Until you meet a better person? A more suitable person? One who isn't…in your debt?"

His jaw jutted, muscles popping. He turned his head and looked out the limo window. The car sailed past tall, elegant homes, mature trees, wide clean sidewalks, wrought-iron gates.

Her eyes burned hot and gritty but she wouldn't cry. She was done crying. "And what if I am pregnant?"

He didn't immediately answer. "Do you think you are?"

"We made love without protection. It could have happened."

Again he didn't speak, not immediately, and the tension grew between them, the silence heavy, suffocating.

Daisy slid off his lap and sat on the seat as far from him as she could manage. Her pride hurt, but her heart felt worse.

As soon as they were back, she'd pack and go. The sooner, the better, too.

Dante briefly glanced at her as the limousine slowed in front of his house but said nothing. Not a word.

She hated him just then, hated him for making her feel so much, want so much, need so much. He'd taken her strength and independence and self-respect, and she had nothing left.

The limousine was parked, yet before the chauffeur could come around Daisy had jumped out and was heading toward the house.

She was trying not to lose control as she ran up the

front steps, but her eyes burned and her throat ached. She hurt all over.

Suddenly a shadow moved near the entry, and Daisy froze. The shadow moved again, stepping away from the potted topiary and into the porch light.

Anabella.

Dante wasn't surprised by Anabella's sudden appearance. Daisy watched his face, and it was as though he knew his sister would be arriving, had expected her arrival tonight, if not sooner.

But how had he known?

Dante caught her staring and turned toward her. His dark eyes raked her, no love lost in his hard expression.

"Have you made your mind up then?" he asked. He couldn't have sounded more indifferent if he'd tried.

If Daisy hadn't made up her mind before, she had now. "Yes." The single syllable thankfully came out resolute. And the moment she'd said it, she knew it was the truth.

"Then don't let me stand in your way."

Just like that, it was over.

Daisy moved to Anabella and hugged her, trying not to meet Anabella's wide apprehensive gaze. The girl had enough problems of her own without needing to worry about one more.

It didn't take long to pack. Daisy hadn't brought many clothes, and most of them were still at the *estancia*. She knew Dante would have them boxed and shipped. Not because they were valuable, but because he wouldn't want the reminder in his house.

She knew him. Knew him better than she thought she'd ever know him.

It would have been easier to leave if they hadn't become intimate. Far easier to say goodbye if her body and heart weren't screaming in protest.

Suitcase in hand, Daisy ventured downstairs. The library doors were shut, and standing outside in the hall, the only sound Daisy could hear was Anabella weeping.

Daisy stood transfixed, unable to move a step in either direction. She couldn't open the door and interrupt, yet she couldn't walk out without saying goodbye.

"Do you know what you've done?" Dante's voice rang out. "Your mother hired mercenaries to find you, mercenaries to track you down. You could have been hurt, Anabella, or worse!"

"What about Lucio? Where is he? What have they done with him?"

"They've done nothing with him."

"Then where is he? He wouldn't just leave me. He loves me. He *loves* me!"

Anabella's cry tore at Daisy's heart. She moved to the door and yet even as her hand reached for the knob she couldn't quite twist it open. How was she going to help the situation?

"But if he loves you, where is he? Why did he run off? How could he do that to you?"

"I don't know, but I'm sure something's happened to him."

"Are you pregnant, Anabella?"

Daisy closed her eyes, held her breath, waiting for the answer.

"I don't know," the girl answered.

"How can you not know? It's quite simple, actually."

"I haven't taken a doctor's test."

"But you're...late."

"Late, yes."

Daisy's chest squeezed tight. If Anabella was pregnant, and if the gaucho was the father, what would Dante want her to do?

What a thing to think! It wasn't Dante's choice. This wasn't about him.

She felt a rise of anger and then stopped herself, realizing she couldn't get involved. This wasn't her family. Dante had made that abundantly clear.

Daisy lifted her suitcase and walked to the front door. As she swung the door open the library door opened, too. Dante stood in the door frame, no hint of emotion or expression on his hard face.

"The car's out front," he said. "I've also arranged a ticket for you. You'll just need to check in at the counter, show identification."

Her chest hurt. "Thank you," she whispered. She looked at him, wondered what else she was supposed to say. She knew the farm still owed him a great deal of money, and their working relationship was far from over, but things between them would be different. It had to be.

But the farm was the important thing, she reminded herself fiercely, even as she wondered if that was still true.

The farm *was* important, but falling in love with Dante had changed her. She felt more deeply, wanted more for herself personally. It wasn't enough to just pour herself into the farm. She wanted to love. To be loved.

But just because she wanted more didn't mean Dante wanted more. She couldn't make him want more. The only thing she could do was go home, focus on the farm, try to get some perspective again.

It was time to go, but Daisy couldn't move. Despite her determination to make the goodbye as clean and as unemotional as possible, she longed to touch Dante one last time, to feel close to him once more.

Which was exactly why she couldn't touch him. If she touched him, she'd never be able to turn around and walk away. Her need for him was a weakness. She couldn't afford to be weak now, not when her family still depended on her.

Abruptly she turned away, even as her heart twisted hard and sharp inside her chest. The pain was so intense it blindsided her, and for one split second she thought she might get sick.

Instead she slid into the back of the waiting car and dug her hands into tight fists, praying she wouldn't break down until the car had pulled away.

And it dawned on her just then, as she was fighting tears and fighting for control, that she'd saved the farm—only to be forever in Dante's debt.

Five and a half weeks after returning from Argentina, Daisy received a letter in the mail.

Daisy recognized the postmark and Anabella's handwriting. Heart pounding, she tore open the envelope.

Dear Daisy, Good news! I've found a new school and

am studying hard to pass my exams at the end of the year. I miss Lucio terribly but am trying to concentrate on my studies. I miss you. Come visit us soon. Kisses, Anabella.

So Anabella wasn't pregnant, after all.

Dante must be quite relieved.

Daisy held the single sheet of stationery in her hands for a long time before slowly folding the page and slipping it into the envelope. She tucked the letter into her top dresser drawer and went to stand at her bedroom window.

How ironic. Anabella wasn't pregnant, but she was. Six weeks pregnant.

CHAPTER ELEVEN

TENDRILS of fog clung to the pasture. It was cold this morning, colder than usual for so early in November, but the stable felt warm and smelled familiar—horses and hay and worn leather.

As Daisy groomed Mimi, she realized that while she still loved the farm, her priorities had changed. She'd discovered that loving Dante made her want more out of life than just horses and chores. She wanted a family. She wanted to be a wife and a mother but couldn't imagine having a family if it wasn't with Dante.

She loved him so much it was impossible to imagine life without him, but what hope had he given her? In seven weeks of being home, she'd heard his voice only once, and that was only because he'd called the farm wanting to speak to Clemente.

She remembered how she'd frozen at the sound of his voice, remembered how tightly she'd clenched the phone, her heart pounding, her stomach falling, and for a split second she almost begged him to come see her. Almost begged him to love her.

Thankfully self-control won and she put down the phone without embarrassing herself and located Clemente.

But that one call, that one brief contact with Dante,

had set her heart on fire all over again. For days after she could hardly eat or sleep. She cursed him, cried for him in private and then slowly resigned herself to a life without him.

The truth was, she might be able to make him talk to her, but she could never make him love her, at least, not love her the way she needed to be loved.

Daisy shook her head, shaking off the memories of the phone call, and reached for Mimi's saddle. But as she lifted the saddle, the weight of it was plucked from her hands.

"Should you be doing that, Señorita Daisy?" Clemente asked, positioning the saddle on Mimi's back.

She froze for a moment, mind racing, and then stooped to grab the strap. "Why not?"

"You know why," he answered respectfully even as he pulled the strap from her, cinching the saddle.

Heat warmed her cheeks. He couldn't know. She hadn't told anyone about the baby yet. Not even Zoe. There was no way Clemente knew. But Clemente's cryptic words stayed with her as she gave the riding lessons, and later, when she headed to the track office to catch up on invoices.

As she stared at the computer screen—getting the farm accounts onto a computer was one of Dante's first changes—Daisy thought again about Clemente's words.

If Clemente did know, would he tell Dante, or did he expect her to tell Dante?

She wanted to tell Dante, but she couldn't forget how Dante had made marriage and children sound like torture, and the last thing she wanted to do was force a child on him. But that didn't mean she'd end the pregnancy or give the baby up. The baby was as much a Collingsworth as it was a Galván, and the Collingsworths were good people, solid people. She was determined to raise the baby here, on the farm, among people she loved.

Her eyes burned, and she glanced at the keyboard but couldn't read any of the keys. She wished Dante could be part of the baby's life, but he'd made his choice and she'd made hers. And that's the way it was.

December arrived without much fanfare. In the Buenos Aires house, Anabella had the stereo blasting again, the bass so loud that the elegant plaster walls were vibrating. But they were vibrating with Christmas carols, not her usual hard rock.

Dante stood before the decorated mantel and stared into the cold hearth. Anabella loved the festive colors and tinsel at Christmas, and if it weren't for her, he would have skipped Christmas this year. He'd never felt less like celebrating.

Daisy should be here. He wanted her here. If he closed his eyes he could see her, picture her opening the door and walking in, all long-legged beauty, fair hair gathered in a loose ponytail, silver-blond tendrils clinging to her cheeks. Her eyes would snap fire, her smile would challenge him, and he'd love her. *He did love her.*

He wanted Daisy, but could he do the traditional marriage, the *niños*, the nice house in the suburbs? Could he be that person for her? And if not, why? What was he afraid of?

Disappointing her. The answer drifted up like a guilty conscience. He was afraid he'd disappoint her the same way his father had disappointed those who loved him.

The way Dante had failed Tadeo.

Tadeo had needed him, and he hadn't been there. And Dante hadn't been there because Tadeo, the little brother who wanted desperately to please, had never asked for help.

Tadeo, the little brother who wanted Dante's admiration more than anything, had been too proud, too determined to handle life on his own...

So what happened?

Tadeo crashed and burned.

Dante felt physically sick. It made him nauseous just remembering, but maybe it was time he faced all the skeletons in the closet. Maybe it was time to confront all the shoulds and woulds that drove him to act, or *not* act, as it happened in Daisy's case.

He stalked to his liquor cabinet, poured a neat Scotch and threw it back in one swallow. The liquor burned his throat but it was a welcome relief from the mocking voice inside his head. At some point he had to stop comparing himself to his father, stop second-guessing himself and just act with confidence. Act on his heart.

Dante reached for the phone, dialed the Collingsworth number, having memorized it from the dozen times he picked up the phone to call but hadn't completed it. This time he let the call go through. "Zoe, this is Dante Galván. Is Daisy there?"

But Daisy wasn't available; she was in town on an errand, seeing the doctor. "Is she all right?"

Zoe hesitated too long. Then Dante knew.

"She's pregnant," he said softly, almost beneath his breath. "She's pregnant and she wasn't going to tell me."

"I didn't say anything!" Zoe protested. "Daisy will be furious—"

"You didn't say anything. I think I always knew."

New Year's Day, it rained all day. In fact, it'd rained for four days straight. Mud caked on Daisy's boots as she tramped from the driveway to the stable. She swung the stable door open and froze. Inside the stable, talking to Clemente, was Dante.

Dante, here. Dante on her farm, in her stable.

Her legs threatened to buckle, and she leaned against the door, fingers pressed on the rough wood.

He was so engrossed in conversation with Clemente that he didn't know she was there, and she watched him with rabid interest. He stood with one foot propped on the water trough, dressed in a blazer, dark shirt and jeans. His hair was longer than the last time she had seen him, and yet he looked better than ever, more handsome, more rugged.

Suddenly Clemente looked up and Dante turned, spotting her in the doorway. In his eyes she saw a flicker of what they'd been to each other, of what they'd meant.

He hadn't forgotten her, not completely.

The realization that he remembered filled her with longing. To be in his arms again…to be part of him again…

Her lips parted. She wanted to say something and then remembered what had driven them apart.

Marriage, family, babies. *Babies*...

Dante walked toward her, closing the distance. Reaching her, he leaned forward and kissed her on both cheeks. The spice of his cologne filled her nose. She pressed her fingers to his blazer, intent on pushing him back, and yet her hand lingered against his jacket, her fingertips almost caressing the wool fabric.

"Daisy."

She felt a bittersweet thrill at the way he said her name. He made her feel so fragile and so beautiful. It was the first bit of tenderness she'd felt in months. "What are you doing here?"

"I came to see you."

"I thought perhaps you were checking on your investments."

His mouth twisted, but it wasn't a smile. "How are you feeling?"

"I'm fine."

"Are you?"

A sixth sense alerted her to danger. She threw her head back to get a better look at his face and saw the somber light in his eyes. "Is that why you're here, to check on my health?"

"Maybe."

"Then you've wasted your time. I'm fine, the farm is fine, everything is fine."

"Of course you'd say that."

"*I* haven't changed," she answered bitterly, far more bitterly than she'd intended. He'd hurt her, she realized yet again, he'd hurt her far more deeply than she'd acknowledged, and she didn't know how to forget, or forgive.

Dante's jaw tightened. "I could use a cup of coffee. Is there any in the office?"

"No." She hadn't been able to stomach coffee since getting pregnant.

"Tea?"

"There's water."

"I'll have some water then."

She cleaned her boots outside the office on the wire brush before heading inside, painfully aware of Dante standing behind her, waiting.

"It's time we talked," he said. He didn't take a seat. "We should have talked a long time ago."

She wished he'd sit down. "What should we have talked about?"

"Daisy, don't play games, not now, not over this. It's too important."

So he did know. She wondered how he found out but didn't have the energy to ask. "You don't want this baby, Dante, don't pretend you do."

"It's not what I would have chosen—"

"Then get out!" She slammed her hands on the desk, interrupting him. "I don't need you here, and I don't need you to interfere."

"Why did I know you'd say that?"

It was the first time he'd ever shouted at her, and she fell silent, shocked. Daisy swallowed, pressed her knuckles against the desk, fought ridiculous tears that had no place in this conversation. "Because it's true," she said huskily. "I'm capable of raising the baby on my own."

"Sorry, *muneca*, but that's not an option. It's my baby, too, and we're going to raise *our* baby together."

"That'll be a little difficult when we live on different continents."

"We'll get married. You'll move back to Argentina with me."

"No way. I'd never marry you now."

"Why not? Two months ago you desperately wanted me to marry you. What's standing in the way now?"

Love, she answered silently, *the fact that you don't really love me, that you're only marrying me out of guilt.* But she didn't say it, she'd never say it.

This wasn't about her ego but about her values, her most basic beliefs. If and when she married, she'd marry for love. "I'm sorry," she said faintly, "but I can't marry you just to give the baby your name."

"You'd be marrying me to give the baby a family."

"A family? How could we be a family? A family isn't about a piece of paper or a gold wedding band, it's about love. And you don't love me. Not the way I need you to love me." Daisy couldn't say more. She felt her throat thicken with silent tears. She couldn't believe she'd just said what she'd said.

Ashamed, she walked out of the office, but he followed immediately and stopped her at her truck. "I'm not going to step aside and fade into the background. I do love you, Daisy."

"I don't believe it. I don't believe you. You're here because you feel guilty. You're here because Tadeo died and Anabella is troubled. You're here because you can't handle one more person weighing on your sensitive conscience!''

Color drained from his face. "You don't know me very well, do you?"

She'd hurt him. She felt it in the way he visibly recoiled, saw it in his eyes, and while she felt badly that she'd hurt him, she knew they had to be honest. "Maybe I don't know you," she answered more gently, "but that's precisely why I can't marry you. You and I don't know how to compromise. We don't know how to be anything but who and what we are. It'd be a mistake marrying. It'd ruin our lives."

He stared at her long and hard. "And the baby?"

"Will be just fine with me."

He didn't answer for a moment. He glanced at the paddock and green pasture before focusing on her again. "I can't accept that."

"You have to."

"No, I don't." He didn't hesitate. "I believe this baby needs both of us, and we're going to do what's right for our child. My father wasn't around for me, and it confused me, it confused me more than I can say. I won't let our child grow up thinking I don't care, because I do care. I care very much. I want this baby to feel loved, and that's the most important thing to me right now—the only important thing right now."

She couldn't argue with that. The baby's needs would have to come first, and at least Dante was looking at the big picture.

She swallowed hard and felt her anger deflate, as well

as some of her resistance. "Okay. We probably do need to talk."

"Thank you." He was calmer, too. "I have meetings tomorrow in Washington, D.C. Why don't you come with me to D.C.? We'll have dinner tonight and talk about this more."

She opened her mouth to protest that she couldn't leave the farm when she realized it was just a farm, and Clemente was doing fine without her. "All right. But I'm not promising anything. We're just talking, right?"

The hotel in Washington was on the edge of Georgetown, not far from the zoo. The trees lining the streets provided vivid contrast to the sprawling red brick building.

After checking into their top floor rooms, Dante took a seat at the antique desk facing the window and began returning phone calls.

Daisy wandered through the four-room suite feeling adrift. It had seemed like a good idea to have some time alone to talk, but now that she was here in the hotel with him, she felt ridiculously vulnerable. Obviously the shock of seeing him hadn't worn off.

But how could it? In less than twelve hours her life changed. She'd gone from months without a word from him to his declaration of love and his insistence that they marry.

It was too much, too sudden, and his change of heart frightened her. Why hadn't he wanted this before? Why couldn't he see himself married to her before she was pregnant? Why did the baby create such an impetus for being together?

Wanting a quiet place to talk, Dante ordered from room service for dinner, but Daisy lost her appetite. She gagged on her filet, and even Dante gave up any pretense of being able to eat.

He pushed aside his plate. "Let's forget food. We're better off talking."

"I don't know if I can."

"Try," he insisted. "We have to be mature about this."

Mature?

He'd sent her home from Buenos Aires with a broken heart and her pride in tatters. He'd sent her home, and he hadn't called and he hadn't written. He'd talked to Clemente but not to her. He'd handled Collingsworth business but ignored her.

The pain splintered in her heart all over again, sharp stabs of awful emotion, the kind of emotion that Daisy couldn't handle. She hated feeling rejected. Hated feeling lost.

Daisy suddenly pictured a little girl in a stiff navy-blue dress wearing black patent shoes and white ankle socks. The little girl with the blond hair was sitting on the floor of her bedroom hugging a plastic horse and the girl was crying great angry tears because her mommy had gone to heaven and wasn't coming back.

Daisy stared at her ivory plate with the cobalt-blue rim. She wasn't four anymore but she still hurt, she still feared rejection, and if Dante could do it once, he'd do it again.

"I'm sorry," she said huskily, shaking her head, feeling her hair slip across her shoulders. "I can't do this. I can't go through this again."

She stood abruptly and moved to push her chair in, and as she did so, she noticed the bright red stain on the cushion.

Daisy stared at the cushion, her brain so blank there was no specific thought, just panic. Wild, huge, loud panic. Like a megaphone of noise—without the noise.

"Dante." She looked at him in shock. "Help."

Dante rushed her to the hospital, but at that point there was nothing anyone could do. The pregnancy, for whatever reason, was over.

Daisy remained at the hospital for a day and then was sent home, given instructions to see her doctor in Lexington in two weeks' time, but otherwise encouraged to resume normal activity as soon as she felt up to it.

Normal activity, she thought, staring sightlessly out the window as the chauffeured limousine drove Dante and Daisy from the Lexington airport to the farm.

What was normal activity? What was even normal anymore?

Dante touched her gently just above her knee. "I'm sorry, Daisy."

She looked away, out the window at the gently rolling hills of emerald green marked by endless white fences. They weren't far from Collingsworth Farm. Another ten minutes at the most. She gripped her hands together, feeling as fragile as crystal. "What about your meetings in D.C.?"

"They'll be rescheduled."

"I'm sorry you missed them."

"It doesn't matter."

She nodded numbly. Her brain felt so slow, so unlike herself. It was impossible to accept that the pregnancy was over. That it could be over so quickly. She, who liked control, craved control, couldn't control anything.

"I want you to come home with me," Dante said. "It would be good for you to have a change of scenery, get some sunshine. It's summer in Argentina and we could go to my beach house—"

"No." It wasn't an option. She felt a bubble of anger rise inside her, filling her chest, pressing against her heart. It hurt to breathe, hurt to think. How could she love someone and hate someone at the same time?

The only reason Dante had come back for her was because she was pregnant, and now the baby was gone. There was nothing keeping them together, no reason for them to continue together.

"Daisy—"

"No."

"You can't run away from us."

Why did he have to do this? Why couldn't he just drop it? There was no baby. He didn't need to keep up the charade. "There's never been an us."

"There's always been an us. From the moment we met, there's been an us, and I'm not going to lose you."

"Too late. Too much has happened."

"I don't believe that. I believe in second chances, and third chances, at least that's what I've tried to teach Anabella. And I'm going to give us as many chances as we need until we get this right."

The limousine pulled up in front of the old farmhouse, and Daisy jumped out before the driver could move. Dante followed her out. She ran up the front steps, and he caught her at the door.

He spun her to face him. "Daisy, I'm sorry, and perhaps I've handled this badly, but now's the time we need to fight to make this work."

"I can't fight anymore," she answered, pulling away from him. She hurt all over. Her head ached. Her stomach cramped. She felt terribly sick. "I'm too tired to keep fighting. I just want to be alone. Please go away, please just go home."

She ignored a startled Zoe in the hallway and dashed upstairs to her room. Daisy shut the door hard and leaned against it weakly, trembling from head to toe.

Her chest felt tight, and hot, gritty tears burned the back of her eyes. As she stood there, her gaze fell on the far corner of her room. It was the same corner she'd huddled in so many years ago, hugging her plastic horse. She'd sat there in her best dress and cried because her mommy had gone to be with the angels, and Daisy was mad at her mommy, and mad at the angels, and mad at God. Daisy's mommy wasn't supposed to leave her. Not ever.

She was still staring at the corner when she heard the limousine start. Daisy stood straight. Dante was leaving. *No!*

Wild, fierce panic flooded her veins. Dante couldn't leave. She loved him. She needed him. He couldn't do this again.

She ran to the window just in time to see the limousine sail down the drive. Daisy banged on the glass and screamed Dante's name. The car kept going.

Sobbing, Daisy tore downstairs, raced to the front door and threw it open—and ran smack into Dante. He stood on the porch with the suitcases at his feet.

"You..." She drew a short, painful breath. "You're here. I thought you left."

The misty winter light highlighted the deep grooves at his mouth and the creases fanning from his eyes. The strain of the past couple weeks was written all over his face. "Where would I go?"

"Argentina?"

"Not without you."

"What if I don't go back with you?"

"Then I'll stay here."

Ludicrous. "In our house?"

"There's room."

"What if I don't want you here?"

"Then I'll wait until you change your mind."

Her eyes burned, and she swallowed around the lump filling her throat. "That could be quite a wait."

"I'll wait forever, if I have to."

His husky voice sent a quiver through her. His voice sounded rough, raspy. He sounded as tired as she felt. Tears pricked the back of her eyes. She was absolutely exhausted. "But there's no baby."

"There'll be others. We have lots of time."

The lump in her throat grew. Her voice came out a croak. "Please don't break my heart again."

He moved toward her, wrapped his arms around her and held her close. "I won't. I promise."

She meant to be strong, meant to resist him, but the warmth in his voice, the tenderness in his touch were doing something to her, catching her up, sweeping her in. If she wasn't careful she'd be lost all over again.

His hands slid around her, down to the small of her back. "I love you, Daisy. We can make this work."

"I'm so afraid—" And it was then she understood what she was fighting, why she was fighting. She wasn't afraid of him, but of herself. Her rough and tough exterior was little more than a sham, a facade to keep people and pain away.

If she didn't get too attached, she wouldn't get hurt. If she didn't risk loving, she wouldn't risk losing. If she didn't need anyone she wouldn't shatter when that person walked away.

It was a protective measure she developed when her mother died, yet it had failed her when she needed it most.

"Don't be afraid of me," he murmured, kissing one cheek and then the other.

His deep grave voice made her eyes prickle all over again. "I do want children," she said. "I want two or three."

"We'll have those children. I promise."

The tears were welling up again. She couldn't see. "Do you mean it?"

"With all my heart, and I have a very stubborn heart."

"Almost as stubborn as mine."

"I didn't want to say it," he answered soberly. "I didn't want you to throw another punch."

"You do have a hard jaw."

He chuckled softly and pressed a kiss to the corner of her mouth. Her tummy did that little flip it did whenever he touched her.

"Kiss me again," she whispered.

"I might not be able to stop."

"Ha! You have amazing control. You resisted me for weeks in Argentina."

"I can't do it anymore," he said, his head dipping, his lips covering hers.

His kiss touched some of her buried pain, drawing it out, bringing it into the open. She was grateful for his arms around her, needing the support as tears rushed to her eyes and her heart turned inside out.

"I wanted the baby," she said against his mouth.

"So did I, and I feel like I failed you. I couldn't do anything at the hospital, couldn't make it better, couldn't stop the pain. It was the worst feeling in the world."

She clasped his face between her hands and kissed him deeply. Knowing that he understood helped. "Please ask me to marry you again. I promise to say yes this time."

His lashes looked suspiciously damp but his smile was pure Dante, the slow, sexy smile that turned her inside out and made her feel incredibly beautiful and very alive.

"Marry me, Daisy. Make love to me, Daisy—"

"Yes."

He kissed her again, passionately, persuasively so that her legs buckled and her fingers dug into his arms for strength. He smelled heavenly and felt heavenly, and this was the only place she wanted to be.

"Where should we marry?" he asked.

"I don't care. I just want to be with you."

He kissed the tip of her nose. "I had no idea just how much you needed me."

Daisy groaned. "I *don't*. I'm not fragile."

"Yes, you are. Just look at you. Tough Daisy Collingsworth is crying again."

To her chagrin, she was crying. Big fat crocodile tears were filling her eyes, spilling down her face. And yet these tears were tears of hope. "I can't believe it! I *am* crying again."

Disgusted, she wiped away the salty tears and then tugged on one of his thick sun-streaked strands of hair. He looked like a lion. Proud, fierce, protective.

All her life she'd been the strong one, the proud one, but she realized she'd found a man who was every bit as strong and proud. Shyly she stood on tiptoe and pressed a kiss to his incredible lips. "All right, listen clearly because I won't say this again. I do need you, Dante Galván, but only a little tiny bit."

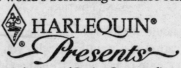

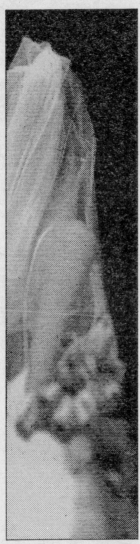

If you enjoyed what you just read,
then we've got an offer you can't resist!

Take 2 bestselling
love stories FREE!
Plus get a FREE surprise gift!

///////////////////////////////

Clip this page and mail it to Harlequin Reader Service®

IN U.S.A.	IN CANADA
3010 Walden Ave.	P.O. Box 609
P.O. Box 1867	Fort Erie, Ontario
Buffalo, N.Y. 14240-1867	L2A 5X3

YES! Please send me 2 free Harlequin Presents® novels and my free surprise gift. After receiving them, if I don't wish to receive anymore, I can return the shipping statement marked cancel. If I don't cancel, I will receive 6 brand-new novels every month, before they're available in stores! In the U.S.A., bill me at the bargain price of $3.57 plus 25¢ shipping & handling per book and applicable sales tax, if any*. In Canada, bill me at the bargain price of $4.24 plus 25¢ shipping & handling per book and applicable taxes**. That's the complete price and a savings of at least 10% off the cover prices—what a great deal! I understand that accepting the 2 free books and gift places me under no obligation ever to buy any books. I can always return a shipment and cancel at any time. Even if I never buy another book from Harlequin, the 2 free books and gift are mine to keep forever.

106 HDN DNTZ
306 HDN DNT2

Name _____ (PLEASE PRINT) _____

Address _____ Apt.# _____

City _____ State/Prov. _____ Zip/Postal Code _____

* Terms and prices subject to change without notice. Sales tax applicable in N.Y.
** Canadian residents will be charged applicable provincial taxes and GST.
All orders subject to approval. Offer limited to one per household and not valid to current Harlequin Presents® subscribers.
® are registered trademarks of Harlequin Enterprises Limited.

PRES02   ©2001 Harlequin Enterprises Limited

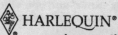

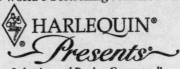